Genial
The Love Song of Simon and Julie

Steve Dewey

An original publication of watwo

Genial
The Love Song of Simon and Julie

Copyright © 2018
Steve Dewey

ISBN: 978-0993222252

http://cometodereham.co.uk
http://www.watwo.me.uk

Cover design: Paul Vought and Steve Dewey

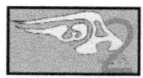

watwo, salisbury, wiltshire, uk

This one's for Deborah, who was there,
and Lizzie, who wishes she had been

*people in pairs, not in a hurry, scuffling, switching their weight
of aestival body, talking casually... the image upon them of lovers*
From *Knoxville, Summer 1915*, James Agee

I may be climbing on rainbows/But baby here goes...
David Gates, Bread, 'Make it With You'

Courting

1

This Covers

THE SUN .

Simon walked up Goldfinch Drive towards home. The afternoon was hot, the sky cloudless, a pale hazy blue, pearly towards the sun. Silver shimmered above the road ahead. There were semi-detached houses on both sides of the road. They were neat, with well-tended front gardens. He'd left Nick and Mark at The White Lion, sitting in the beer garden, still drinking. Simon couldn't afford another drink, and found the hot sun enervating. He had wanted to move, to stretch his limbs, and so had decided to wander home, where he could read a book in the shade.

At the top of Goldfinch Drive, just before he turned into Magpie Road where he lived, Simon found Chris and Gray

5

leaning against the front left wing of a black '68 Triumph Vitesse. The car belonged to Gray. They were in the drive of his parent's large house. Chris saluted as Simon approached. Simon slowed. 'Hello, chaps. What's happening?'

'Nothing,' Chris said.

'Nothing *yet*,' Gray added.

'Yet? You have a plan then?'

'Could be, could be,' Gray said. 'We thought we might go for a drive.'

'Where?'

'Anywhere,' Chris said.

Gray nodded, eyes closed.

'So why are you still standing here?'

'Petrol,' Gray said. 'We only have enough petrol to take us to Southleigh and back again. And we have no money.'

'Well, I do have about fifty pence in my pocket,' Chris said.

'I want to *drive*,' Gray said. 'It's hot, and I've got a soft-top. I want to feel the wind in my hair and a breeze in my face.'

Chris nodded along the road. 'It's Julie,' he said.

Simon and Gray turned to look. A young woman approached. Her hair was blonde, shoulder-length, straight, parted in the middle. She wore jeans, Jesus boots and a tee-shirt. She looked, Simon thought, rather lovely in the sun.

'Can't you borrow some money from your mum and dad?' Simon said.

Gray shook his head. 'Kiddies have gone away. On holiday. Torquay.'

'Oh! Great,' Simon said. 'A party!'

'No chance.'

Julie drew level with them. 'Hello there. So there's a party?'

'No,' Gray said.

'His parents never forgave him for the last one,' Chris said. 'They threatened to sell the car.'

'No matter,' Simon said. 'Mark's having a party soon. His kiddies are away. And he's not a big baby, unlike Gray.'

Gray shrugged. 'I love my car. That's all that matters.'

Julie turned to Simon. She had narrowed her eyes against the glare, but still they shone a bright blue. They sparkled in the sun. 'I thought I saw you in town, drinking with Mark and Nick and Gaz.'

'You did. But they wanted to drink some more. I was too hot. I met these two likely lads on the way home. They were idling.'

'Do you have any money, Jules?' Gray said.

Julie slid her hand into her pocket and withdrew the only coins she had – two ten pence coins and a five pence piece. 'Not even enough for ten Number Six.'

'Here, have one of mine,' Chris said. He offered Julie a cigarette, and lit it with a match.

Julie stood next to Simon. The four of them leaned against the flank of the car, in the hot sun. Simon closed his eyes to shut out the dazzling light.

'So where's Tim?' Gray said.

'We've fallen out,' Julie said. 'I haven't seen him for a while.'

'How long will *this* separation last?' Simon said.

Julie blew smoke up into the blue sky, tilted her head back, and smiled at Simon. 'Don't pretend to be interested. I'll talk to Sarah about it later.'

'Thank goodness for that,' Chris said. 'After all, we have weighty matters to consider. So how much *have* we got between us? Julie, do you want join us? Put your twenty-five pence in the kitty?'

'Sorry, I need my money,' Julie said.

'I've only got fifty pence,' Simon said. 'And I need all of it for a class.'

'Oh, come on,' Gray said. 'Why go to a class during the summer when you don't have to?'

'It's kung fu.'

'Oh yes,' Gray said, and acted scared. 'Forget I said anything. *Ahem.*'

'Don't you two have any money, then?'

'I'll need another pack of fags,' Chris said.

Gray shrugged, and pouted. 'And I have some money, but I need to make it last for the week.'

They were all silent again. There was no pressure to speak. They all knew each other, acquaintances of old. They had grown up in the same town, the same streets, the same schools. None was the other's best friend, not all moved in the same social circles, but they would all be at the same parties, the same pubs, they would share tables when drinking, and friends of friends dated friends of friends. They were all part of the same loose confederacy. They were eighteen and nineteen years old. They had few responsibilities. None of them needed to be anywhere. It was the middle of their summer break. They could relax together in the heat. And now Julie was here, Simon realised he no longer wanted to go home.

Simon turned to Gray. 'Where's your mother's car?'

Gray nodded towards the garage. 'In there.'

'Has anybody thought,' Simon ventured, 'to syphon petrol out of the Mini?'

Gray looked at Chris. 'You're the mechanical brains of this outfit. Can we do that?'

Chris's round face broke into a grin. 'Well, yes, we can. Simon, that's brilliant. If you smoked, I'd give you a fag or two. Julie, give him a kiss.' Julie dropped her cigarette onto the driveway. She scraped it across the asphalt under her sandal, and then kissed Simon on the cheek. She smelled of tobacco, and scent and soap.

'I suppose,' Chris said, 'I'm only one who knows how to syphon a fuel tank?'

Gray looked at Simon. 'Well, do *you* know how?'

Simon shook his head. 'I have no idea.'

'I know how to do it,' Julie said. 'But *you* should know I'm not going to.'

'No, she's not,' Simon agreed. 'She smells of soap and sunshine, and should remain that way.'

'Quite right,' Julie said, lazily, softly. She had turned her face up to the sun and closed her eyes. Her skin remained pale despite the long summer days of sunshine. She would always be pale, Simon supposed. She wouldn't tan, she would become at most more pink. Gray and Chris were brown. Simon suspected that Gray might even have been sunbathing.

'It's down to me then, I suppose,' Chris said. 'I bloody hate the taste of petrol.'

'If you succeed, I'll get you a beer or two,' Gray said.

'I need some tubing.'

Gray said there might be some in the garage, and led Chris away.

Simon looked at Julie. She leaned against the Vitesse, her eyes closed, drinking in the sun. 'If you're not seeing Tim, come to the Lion tonight and see us.'

Simon and his friends drank in The White Lion. Julie's haunt was The Swan, as Tim preferred it.

'Perhaps. Depends. Depends on...' She trailed off.

'Depends on Tim?'

She sighed. 'I suppose so. Does that make me pathetic?'

'Yes. A bit. Go on, come down the Lion. Brighten things up.'

Julie opened her eyes then, and looked at Simon. 'Would I brighten things up?'

'Of course you would. We've missed you since you started hanging out with Tim.'

Julie had been much closer to Simon and his friends a year or so ago, before Tim. She closed her blue eyes again. There was a faint smile on her lips. 'It would be nice to be with you all. Can I?'

It wasn't as if Julie *never* came to The White Lion any more. She even brought Tim along sometimes. Yet Simon sensed now that Julie needed reassurance, she needed to know her old friends were still there for her. 'Of course you can. We'd love to see you.'

Chris and Gray stumbled around behind the garage door,

opening drawers and cupboards, closing them again, clattering toolbox lids back into place, and muttering, laughing and cursing.

'What happened with Tim?'

'Oh, you know, boy and girl stuff.'

'I know little about that boy and girl stuff. I only know what I hear from you. And from Imo, and Chrissie. Oh, and Kate. And... you know...'

Julie turned to look at him again, the smile still on her lips. 'I do know. And that's quite a list of lovelies there.'

Simon shrugged. 'Girls talk to me. They think I'm safe.'

'You are, Si,' Julie said. She put her arm through his and leaned against him.

Simon found it difficult to believe that he was attractive to women. He'd never yet had a girlfriend. He knew that girls liked to be around him; he was attentive. He made them laugh. He offered a shoulder to cry on. 'I'm shy with girls,' he said.

'That is nonsense, Si,' Julie said. 'You might be a bit wary of us girls, but only because you don't understand the going-out-together thing. They might frighten you a bit, at the moment. You might not be ready for a girlfriend. But believe me, you are *not* shy with us.'

Simon made no reply. He remembered Anna, his friend at Southleigh College, who had, perhaps, wanted to be more than a friend. She was funny, bright, pretty. At the Summer Ball – the last day before the long summer break, the last day he and Anna would be in college together for eight weeks or more – she'd said he was *really* nice. She liked him. And that had confounded Simon, whose only words had been *thank you*. Which had been the wrong thing to say, he knew. He should, perhaps, have done more, said more. But he never expected girls to like him. He'd spent the last six weeks thinking about Anna. Did she still think about him? Did she want to go out with him? Would she still be interested in him in another month? Simon hoped she would. But eight weeks was a long time when you're eighteen, and he had no way of contacting Anna – because, although he and Anna had spent three months together, laughing and joking with each other, they'd never thought to ask each other for telephone numbers and addresses. Certainly, Simon would never have asked; after all, women weren't interested in him in that way.

'Tim is turning into a pig,' Julie said. 'He was all attentive when we first got it together. We went places, did things together. But now he spends more time hanging out with his friends, and going over to Bath on Saturday nights with them and not me.'

'Chrissie says the same about Jake,' Simon said. They both knew who Chrissie and Jake were, and their problems. 'Perhaps it's the way all relationships go.' Although his wouldn't, Simon thought, if he were ever lucky enough to have one, if Anna still felt the way he hoped she did.

'I noticed you were a bit thick with Chrissie.'

'Yeah, for a while.'

'How did Mark take it?'

Mark was one of Simon's best friends and had had a crush on Chrissie for two years. That she had gone out with Jake had not diminished Mark's devotion. 'Mark knew he couldn't talk to her about Jake. It would be too confusing.'

'That's as may be,' Julie said. 'But she seemed very... sparkly... around you.'

'Did she?'

'She did. Didn't you notice? Weren't you tempted to... ask her out?'

'No. There's Mark, and then there's Jake. There's a whole world of complication... And... You think she fancied *me*?'

'Maybe.'

Chrissie, sparkly? Perhaps he was, after all, a bit of a flirt. He wasn't *trying* to be one. He didn't know *how* to be one. But recently, other girls had said it about him. Imogen and Kate had said he flirted, and now Julie also suggested it. But he was,

11

he had always thought, a bit silly, immature, unattractive. All the girls he had liked, including Julie, had gone off with other men. This had further convinced him he didn't look right, that he was somehow unappealing. He had never been upset about it. He knew he wasn't *repellent* or anything. He hoped somebody might one day peer through the patina of plainness and into the core of him, where they'd find... Well, something a woman *might* find attractive. Which is why the thing with Anna had been such a surprise. It wasn't until later, when travelling home from the Summer Ball with his friends, he had realized what had happened, what Anna had been saying and doing. Simon's more mature and experienced friends – Nick, Mark, Danny, James – had all pointed out what was now obvious. Anna really liked him. And he had liked Anna. But as the girls he liked went off with other boys, he'd learned to rein in his feelings. He'd said nothing to Anna that might have caused either of them embarrassment. He wanted to tell Anna what he felt. But he couldn't. He only knew she was Anna, and that she lived somewhere across the border, in Somerset. Not much to go on.

'I always think I'm unattractive,' Simon said.

Julie raised an eyebrow. 'Really? You berk.' She put her head on his shoulder.

Chris and Gray came back. Both carried a milk bottle in each hand. 'Man the barricades,' Gray said. 'I'm starting a riot, right here.'

'Oh, don't do that,' Julie sighed. 'It's too hot.'

Chris breathed on Julie. 'Give us a kiss.'

Julie pulled at Simon's arm, and brought her body tighter into his. 'No. You smell like... like... an overflowing carburettor.'

'Oh, get you,' Chris laughed. He followed Gray to the back of the car, where they poured their petrol into the tank of the Vitesse.

Simon squinted towards Gray. 'How many miles to the gallon does this thing get?'

Gray shrugged. 'About twenty five, I suppose.'

Julie was still leaning against Simon. He rather liked it. 'And what is four pints?'

'A lot of milk?' Gray said. 'Oh, oh, something to do with a compass? No, wait. Johnny Four Pints, the gangster from Salisbury. He's quite small, four pints short of a gallon.'

'Almost,' Simon said. 'Four pints is indeed four short of a gallon. So that's half a gallon. So that's about twelve miles of fun.'

'Twelve miles of fun sounds like a lot,' Gray said.

'It'd get us from here to Southleigh and back,' Chris said. 'About twenty minutes driving.'

'Oh. Bugger it,' Gray said. He looked at Chris. 'Oh, well, you'd better get sucking again.'

Chris's narrow shoulders slumped. 'Damn. Must I?'

'Yes, you don't get any beer until your work is done.'

'But I don't want to suck.'

Gray smiled. 'But you *do* suck.'

They walked away, clutching their bottles, bickering as they went down the path by the side of the garage – Gray demanding more petrol, Chris demanding his beers – and disappeared through the side door. Simon leaned his cheek against Julie's head. Her blonde hair smelled of Vosene and sunshine. He was tempted for a moment to kiss it, but then the moment passed. Sun warmed them. They leaned against each other, waiting for Gray and Chris to return with the fuel. He could hear the muffled voice of Chris, then Gray, behind the blue metal garage door. Sometimes, he could hear them giggling. Simon wondered if Julie would come to the White Lion this evening. He supposed she would go to The Swan, though. She had been with Tim for a year. Would she resist seeking him out, showing herself off, or reconciling? Could she resist making him jealous? Julie would be better off coming to the Lion. And seeing him.

Chris and Gray returned, their bottles clinking. They both smelt dangerously flammable. 'Don't smoke,' Simon said to Julie.

Chris frowned. 'That is the last syphoning I'm doing for the day. The only thing entering my mouth now is booze and a fag or two.'

'Booze first, then, I would suggest,' Julie said.

Chris and Gray poured the fuel into the tank of the Vitesse. They put their bottles down on the drive. 'I don't think the milkman wants them now,' Gray mused. He squinted at Simon. 'Do the maths thing, Si. How far can we go?'

'Well, there must have been a little fuel in there to start with. And you added, what, twenty-five or thirty miles? So perhaps then we could travel thirty or forty miles. Not to the beach and back, that's too far.'

'But who wants to come back?' Gray said.

'I do,' Simon said. 'There's sausages for tea tonight.'

'Stonehenge,' Julie said. 'Let's go touch the stones.'

'Excellent idea,' Gray said. 'Let's get all mystical, man.' He made a peace sign, and then opened the door of the Vitesse. He slipped onto the leather driver's seat, and turned the ignition key. The straight six spluttered into life. 'Yes!' Gray exclaimed. He looked at each of them. The engine ticked over smoothly. 'Well, come on then! We've got twelve miles to drive, the sun is up, the rest of the day is set warm and fair, and we need to feel the wind in our hair.'

'My word,' Chris said. 'How very poetic.'

The soft top of the Vitesse was down. Simon climbed over the panel behind Gray and sat on the red leather bench seat.

Julie walked around to the passenger door.

'Would you like to sit in the front?' Chris said.

'You stinky boys should sit together.' She looked at Simon. 'I'll just snuggle up on the back seat with Si.'

Chris tilted the passenger seat forward so Julie could slide next to Simon. 'Hello, shy boy,' she said.

As soon as Chris sat down and shut his door, Gray crunched the gearbox into reverse and threw everybody forward as he accelerated backwards from the drive into the road. He braked hard, throwing everybody backwards; they remained pinned in their seats as he crunched the car into first gear and accelerated down Goldfinch Drive towards the junction with Barton Road. 'The synchromesh is going,' Gray said, in a feeble attempt to explain away his jarring gear changes.

He screeched to a halt at the junction, and then squealed out onto Barton Road, heading out of town and away into the countryside. The engine rasped seductively as Gray accelerated. 'Brilliant,' he laughed.

'We must get you a woman,' Julie said. 'You're enjoying this car far too much.'

As Gray pushed the Vitesse up to sixty the wind rushed over and around the windscreen and took Julie's words with it. 'What?' Gray said.

Simon's long fair hair flew around his face. He pushed it back behind him, trying to keep it from getting in his eyes and mouth. He looked at Julie. Her blonde hair also blew out of control, fine strands flying in all directions. She was looking at him, her blue eyes sky-coloured and shining with the sun.

'How about you, Si? Do you need a woman?'

'I don't know about *need*. When you've grown up thinking no girl likes you in that way, you kind of think it won't happen anyway, so you don't really think about it at all.'

'I think you need one.'

'Well, I'm open to suggestions.'

Julie smiled mysteriously and then looked down the road. 'I'd have a fag,' she said, 'but this wind would pluck it from my mouth.'

Simon looked at her mouth. Something, somewhere, stirred; and the world became even sunnier. Julie reached over and stroked away some stray, wandering hair from Simon's cheek.

'So what about you?' Simon said. 'Will you ever get over Tim?'

She nodded. 'I should jolly well hope so, I'm only eighteen. I managed to get over Tony when I was only sixteen-and-a-half. I'm a veteran, you see.'

'Tony? Tim? Do I see a pattern here?'

'Yes, I need to move on from the Ts.'

'Oh, I've never thought of you as a tease.'

Julie laughed. 'Oh, I'm not, Si, believe me.' And then her hair flew everywhere again.

Simon glanced over Gray's shoulder at the speedometer. It showed eighty miles an hour. They were heading across Salisbury Plain, dropping down a long straight towards Shrewton. The fields either side of them were unhedged, studded with copses, single tall trees, stunted shrubs, and thickets of gorse. The grass, dry from long days of sunshine, was brown, and scarred by the tracks of tanks, and ruts made by Alvis Stalwarts and Land Rovers. Intermittent signs warned the unwary, who might otherwise wander too deep into unfenced areas of the Plain, of the dangers of unexploded ordnance. They headed towards a tank-crossing, after which the road rose up a short, steep hill.

'Hold on! Here we go!' Julie said.

The car raced over the crossing and up the rise, which they quickly crested before heading downhill again.

Julie put her hands on her stomach, threw her head back, and laughing, shouted 'Yes!' She tousled Gray's thick dark hair.

'I'm glad you're enjoying this,' Chris shouted across the wind. 'But I fixed the bloody suspension last week.' He glared at Gray, who continued to wear the smile that had creased his face since they'd turned into Barton Road.

'You did an excellent job,' Gray said. 'It's sticking to the road like glue.'

They approached the junction near Shrewton too fast. The tyres squealed as they rounded the sharp bend that preceded it. Gray quickly glanced from side to side and let the car roll across the junction. Fortunately, there was little traffic on this hot, lazy day.

Julie had fallen over onto Simon, who had put his arm around her to protect her. 'Thank you, kind sir,' she said.

Gray gunned the car through Shrewton, and then up and down the hills the other side of the village. Soon they could see the grey stones standing and scattered on the Plain. Gray parked the Vitesse in the carpark.

Simon stood up on the back seat. 'Come on!'

Gray looked at the stones, across the road. 'We can see them from here. That'll do me.'

'But we're here now,' Julie said. 'Let's walk over.'

'After all the effort to get petrol in the car, I'm not ruddy well walking.'

'Ruddy well? What are you, forty years old?' Simon said.

'I wanted to feel the wind in my hair!' Gray said.

'At last, I can have a fag,' Chris said. He offered one to Julie, and lit her cigarette, and then his.

Simon sat back down. 'Woh! Mind you don't explode,' he said, and laughed.

'I'm fine,' Chris said. 'The draught has blown the fumes away.'

'How disappointing,' Gray said. 'I was looking forward to your wiry hair flaring up.'

'We should get close to the stones while we're here,' Simon said.

'I'm staying here with Gray,' Chris said, blowing smoke out into the hazy day.

Simon and Julie climbed out over the sides of the car, walked across the car park and crossed road. Barbed-wire fencing had been installed atop the boundary fence, a barrier against the hippies that had descended for the free festival at Summer Solstice. Simon had gone to the festival, which had been held in woodland a mile away, with Chris and Nick, and James and Imogen. They'd spent the night there, people-watching, looking at the stalls, listening to bad music. The scents of patchouli and sandalwood had followed them everywhere. There were spice islands between the trees where curry and chilli bubbled in pans, and clearings from which wafted the homely smells of chips and hot Bovril drinks.

Julie looked at the stones. 'What *are* they for?'

'Well,' Simon said. 'Some people think it's a big astronomical computer.'

'Really?' Julie said.

'The stones are arranged so that can you see the progress of the year by the aligning them with planets and stars in the sky.'

Julie looked at the stones more intently. 'Really?' she said again.

'For example, from the centre of the circle, the sun rises over the Heel Stone at solstice sunrise.'

Julie looked along the fence. 'That's the stone down there, right?'

Simon nodded. 'Yes, that's the one.'

'That's amazing. What else?'

'Well, this guy Gerald Hawkins, he used a computer to check the alignments of the stones with the sun and moon, and planets, and discovered some interesting things.'

'What kind of things?' Julie asked, eagerly.

Simon wished he'd read the rather dull *Stonehenge Decoded* rather more carefully. 'I can't remember them all off the top of my head. There was one other thing though I thought was most interesting. This guy Hawkins thought that you could predict lunar eclipses by moving markers from one Aubury hole to another.'

'So what are Aubury holes then, Si?'

Simon was beginning to struggle with barely remembered facts from a hastily read book. He tried to buy some time. 'I think we should head back to the car.'

'I suppose we should. Gray will be getting bored.'

'Yes. Impatient to move. He does, after all, need the wind in his hair.'

Julie laughed. As they walked slowly back to the car, Simon recalled something from a school trip. 'The Aubury holes are chalk pits,' he said. 'About fifty of them. They follow the ditch.'

They arrived back beside Gray's car.

'So I'm now bored.' Grey said. 'What shall we do?'

'Let's go to the top of Beacon Hill,' Chris said.

'I don't know,' Simon said. 'That's another three miles there, another three miles back...'

'Sod that,' Gray said, 'We're going. There must have been a bit of petrol in the tank before we added more.'

'On your own head be it,' Julie said. 'I'm not pushing.'

'Tish,' Gray said. 'It'll be fine.'

Julie and Simon climbed into the back. Gray started the Vitesse. The car squealed away from its parking space and squealed around the car park, then squealed left and headed for the A303.

'Hold onto your hats,' Julie said, smiling as her hair once more danced around her face.

'I don't have one,' Simon said.

'We should hold onto Gray's hair,' Chris shouted. 'It looks like a bonnet.'

Gray smiled, but he'd been smiling since he started the car. It was true, Simon thought. Gray's bowl-shaped cut and dark hair resembled some old-fashioned bonnet. They were now on the A303, heading towards the Countess roundabout, which Gray took with his usual speed.

Simon slid over into Julie. 'Pardon me, madam,' he said. He slid back again as Gray flung the car in the opposite direction.

They began the long ascent up the dual carriageway towards Beacon Hill. Chris pointed ahead, at the gateway to a field, set back from the road. Gray slowed and pulled onto the grass. Dust from the dry soil lifted around them, and then slowly drifted away on the barely-there breeze. They all exited the car again.

At the summit of the hill, there were metal aerials and telegraph poles. Something to do with the military, Simon supposed. They climbed over the gate and walked up a track, to a spot where the view was better. They sat on the grass. Julie was next to Simon, as she had been all afternoon. She had a cigarette in her mouth, one of her own. She had offered one to

Chris but he had politely declined, knowing she had few left and little cash until Saturday. Julie leaned her head against Simon's shoulder. Sweet cigarette smoke mingled with soap and shampoo scents. They could hear cars speeding by on the road below them, but it was early evening now, and the rush hour, such as it was in Wiltshire in late summer, had passed.

Simon looked at the heat-hazed countryside around him. The fields were dotted with drooping hawthorn and gorse bushes. The summit of Beacon Hill blocked his view to the north and east. To the south, west and north-west were views over Wiltshire and Hampshire. He could see Bulford Camp, Bulford village, Amesbury and Boscombe Down aerodrome. He heard a jet engine, and scanned the skies to the east. He caught sight of a Jaguar approaching the runway. The Jaguar was still a new shape to him. He had grown up watching Buccaneers, Phantoms, and Lightnings scream over the Plain.

There were still three hours until sunset. The air was sultry. Simon was late for tea. His mum would leave the plate of whatever food she had cooked – sausages, he remembered – in the oven to keep warm. There would, of course, be disapproval. Out here in the warm evening – where fields and hills rolled away to a horizon obscured by a blue veil of heat-haze that softened the shapes and edges of trees and buildings, where jets screamed into Boscombe, where hidden distances held the secrets of tomorrow's adventures, where Julie's head on his shoulder offered a frisson of promise – disapproval was a distant discomfort he could easily endure.

They relaxed and watched the sun, the traffic, the hazy distances. Chris and Julie smoked. There was desultory talk – the upcoming party at Mark's, who it was that Sarah fancied, what Imogen would do if James continued drinking, would Chrissie split with Jake again, and if so what would Mark do.

Finally, Chris said, 'We need to move on.'

They lazily stood, dusted themselves down, walked back along the track, climbed the gate and entered the car again.

Wheels spun and grit flew as they headed onto the A303 and accelerated towards the roundabout a mile east. Tyres and rear-seat occupants complained as they were flung around the roundabout. Then they headed up the hill again towards Stonehenge, the wind buffeting them all.

Conversation slowed. Julie turned, leaned her back against the side panel and put her legs on Simon's lap. She tilted her head back, her blonde hair crazy with speed. Simon wasn't sure, as ever, what he should do when unexpected random intimacies, such as Julie's legs in his lap, occurred. He gingerly rested his hands on those legs, stroked them a little. He never ventured beyond the knee. Simon's eyes sometimes met Julie's, and her eyes were as bright and sunny as the day.

As they sped along the hot, black, tar-weeping roads into Dereham, Simon thought he could hear an odd noise from the engine, a soft grating, or a muffled whine. At last, they arrived back in Goldfinch Drive. With a final suffering squeal, the car stopped just an inch short of the garage door.

Simon patted Julie's legs. 'Honey, we're home.'

'Shame,' Julie said, and slowly lifted her legs from Simon's lap. Simon stood in the footwell, and offered her his hand. She took it and Simon pulled her up.

Once outside the car, Julie hugged Gray, then Chris. 'It's been fun,' she said. Then she hugged Simon.

'Come down the Lion tonight,' Simon said.

'We'll see,' Julie said. She squeezed Simon tight for a moment, and then let go. 'I'll see you guys soon,' she said. She gave a little wave, and then walked back down Goldfinch Drive.

Simon turned and found Gray's brown eyes on him, an eyebrow raised. Gray had no need to say anything; Simon knew what that eyebrow meant. Indeed, Simon would raise an eyebrow at himself, if he could.

Gray then turned to Chris, frowning. 'What was that racket coming from the engine?'

Chris shrugged. 'I'm not sure. A piston ring? Let's not worry too much about it now.'

'I'd like to stay and help,' Simon said.

'Liar,' Gray said, laughing.

'That's true.

I must get home and see what burnt offering awaits me in the oven. Thanks for the fun.'

Simon walked away, leaving Gray and Chris as he had found them four hours ago: leaning against the flanks of the black Vitesse.

He turned into Magpie Road, thinking of Julie. Julie in the sun. Julie with crazy wind-blown hair. Julie smiling, her blue eyes sparkling. Julie's head on his shoulder. The scent of cigarettes, of soap and shampoo.

2

This Crosses

WHEEL of FORTUNE.

Julie's walk was slow, leisurely as she headed into town. She had no plan. She'd rung Sarah's house but there had been no answer. Then she had dared ring Simon, but nobody answered there, either. She had only for a moment contemplated ringing Tim before dismissing the idea. She'd inveigled a little more money from her parents, which she would have to pay back tomorrow. She had bought ten Number Six at the newsagents, and had enough left over to buy a drink or two.

The afternoon was hot. The sun shone as bright as it always did. She wore jeans, tee-shirt, and Jesus boots again, as she had seemed to for most of the summer. Sometimes she despaired of the heat and wondered if it would go on forever. Most of the time, though, she simply enjoyed the strange and pervasive Mediterranean ambience. Everybody wore tee-shirts and jeans, or floaty, strappy, dresses from Laura Ashley and Miss Selfridge. Some of the freakier girls wore halter-tops and skirts. When evening arrived, people drank outside of pubs, stood in the streets, smoked and chatted, and beer gardens were, for a change, full and lively. Older people prepared salads which they ate in their gardens with cold drinks and then ice cream later. Younger people hung their heads from open car windows, out of which issued music, thin and tinny. They held their palms up against the breeze as the cars moved, seeking relief from the ever-present heat.

Julie looked at the clock on the side of St Peter's church tower. Five past one. The pubs stayed open for another hour or so yet. She recalled what Simon had said. She should go to the White Lion. She hadn't gone last night because... Well, because she had no money, and because she had no desire to inadvertently meet Tim. Being with Simon, Chris and Gray yesterday had been so lovely, she had felt so very relaxed, she had been determined not to end the day with a chance meeting. In the evening she had instead watched some television with her parents and her sister, and then gone to her bedroom to listen to Carole King and James Taylor, and to read her book. Today, Tim would be at his work in Southleigh, so she could now enjoy the sun, and enjoy Simon's company again if she could find him.

She crossed over the dusty road and headed for The White Lion. The pub sat at the centre of a crescent of shops that curved around the old Market Place. She walked up the steps, through the door and headed for the saloon bar. Simon wasn't there, but Simon's friend Mark was. He chatted with two other people Julie knew, the lovely Imogen and James. She bought a cold Coca Cola. When she turned, Mark waved her over.

'Nice to see you,' he said as she sat on the stool next to him.

'Simon suggested I come here more often,' Julie said. 'Is he around? Have you seen him today?'

'No, he's gone walking with Stuart, over the hills and far away. Fitness freaks, the pair of them.'

Simon did kung fu and tai chi; Stuart played badminton and walked. It was not at all unusual for them to take a long hike out over hill and down together. Oh well. She'd sit here and find out what had been happening in the world of Mark, James and Imogen.

'It's too hot for all that madness,' Mark said. 'That's why I have a bike.'

Mark had a motorbike, a Honda. Julie often saw him on it.

'I thought it was, uh, to pull chicks,' James said. He was drinking brandy, as ever. James worked in Bentons – Dereham's only department store – at weekends, and had generous amounts of pocket money from his well-to-do parents.

Mark sighed, and then frowned. 'There's only one chick I want to pull,' he said.

Everyone knew who he meant, so nobody said anything.

Julie looked at James. 'Can I just say your beard gets more ridiculous every time I see it.'

James's beard was most extravagant for a young man. Imogen laughed. 'To the point, as always, Julie,' she said.

'But it is! He's turning into a bloody caveman I tell you.'

James had been a fast developer, and had needed to shave before any of his friends, sometimes turning up in the fifth year at school with a faint five o'clock shadow. His hairiness had only increased during sixth-form as he had become more of a freak. He had grown his dark hair until it reached his shoulders, and trained the beard that had so soon sprouted from his chin into a full but unkempt Edwardian bush.

'Shaving is so bourgeois,' James said, always quick to separate himself from the middle-classes, and hoping – while drinking brandy, pocketing the money from his parents, and reading Eliot – that he somehow connected with the concerns of the working class. He finished his glass of Martell. 'Ready, Mark?'

Mark swigged down his half of bitter, and then nodded.

James turned to Imo. 'Are you coming with us?'

Imo shook her head. 'Poor Jules has only just arrived. I'll stay and chat with her a while.'

James kissed Imo's cheek. He put on his square-framed sunglasses, and then both he and Mark said goodbye.

'Where are they off to?' Julie said.

'Oh, James has written some lyrics for Honeyhouse. Mark is going to take a look at them. They'll talk about the band all afternoon.'

Mark played bass in Honeyhouse, and James wrote lyrics for them. Julie had seen the band a few times. They were a bit too progressive for her liking, although they could rock out. She had even danced to the rockier songs, when drunk.

'So,' Julie said. 'I see you and James have got together again?'

Imogen nodded. 'Yes. Kind of. We'll see how it goes this time.'

'And you split because?'

'The drink. The drugs.'

Julie was surprised. 'He's not that bad, is he?' She recalled the most drug-addled fool she knew. 'He's hardly Greaser, after all.'

Imogen frowned. 'Oh, I know that. And to be honest it wasn't the drugs that were bothering me so much as the booze. To see James tucking back a quart of brandy every day was... disconcerting.'

'A quart?'

'Yes. He was so often drunk when I met him in the evening his boyish stumbling lost its charm.'

'Well, it's not like he's an alkie. He can stop, right? He's slowed down for you.'

'I hope he's doing it for himself.' Imogen sighed. 'So, yes, he's not an alcoholic. You're right there. But he was drinking so much he soon would be. And if he was so easily addicted to booze, you have to wonder how long it would be before it was cocaine.'

'Coke?'

'Yes, of course, he's tried it. As he always says, you have to try these things. Although I think his philosophical justifications for taking drugs are only poor excuses for getting smashed.'

Julie's acquaintance with the more sordid end of the desire to 'chill out', and 'lay back', and 'be cool', and 'party' was through the denizens of The Swan – Dodgy Len, Greaser, and some of Tim's friends, who were five or more years older than she was. Certainly Greaser looked older than his twenty-three years, grubby somehow, tired. Greaser's girlfriend, Jan, was always frowning, already lines showed on her pretty young face.

'But he's stopped with the coke, now, right?' Julie said.

'Right. Martell or coke, but not both. Not with me, anyway. He chose a little Martell, and me.'

'So that's got to be good.'

'I suppose so.' Imogen slumped in her chair. Julie rarely saw her like this. Imogen played with the faience bead on the leather cord of her hippie necklace. She looked blankly through the windows into the bright street. Julie felt sorry for her. Normally, she either envied Imogen or stood in awe of her. Imo was five feet eight inches tall and slender, with big cocoa-brown eyes and a mop of extravagant, hennaed curls that tumbled down past her shoulders. Many of the boys and men Julie knew had desired Imo, and she also knew some girls who'd had crushes on her when younger. Imo was confident, intelligent, and graceful. She could sing, and wrote poetry. Imogen was Julie's nightmare, the kind of woman she wanted to be when she looked in a mirror, but found she wasn't. Imogen was, however, too nice to hate – she was friendly, empathetic, and always interested. Julie wouldn't like to see her as drawn and worried as Jan was now.

Imogen spoke again. 'I just hope he's not drinking now, you know? Or rolling a joint. It's a fine excuse, with Mark there. I don't want to control him. But I don't want him off his head all the time.'

Julie nodded. Imogen was obviously worried. It was unusual to see concern in one so young for one so young. Did she fear a dismal future? Perhaps Imo too could see James as Greaser and herself as Jan. Watching James become a Greaser would be very sad, Julie thought. Despite the ridiculous beard, James was slight and fey, only a little taller than a bare-footed Imo. His feminine good looks had cast a spell over many of Dereham's young women, but James had always, it seemed, been destined for Imo. He was probably the brightest boy of their generation, with a great future ahead of him. James wrote too – poems and lyrics for the band, and short stories. It was easy to imagine James on television, talking about his new novel with Melvyn Bragg, or on the road with Honeyhouse, the intellectual lyricist, the band spokesman, his thoughts quoted in New Musical Express, his photograph on magazine covers, he and his beautiful wife in their beautiful home in Wiltshire, their faces splashed across pages of *Tatler* or *Cosmo* or *Vogue*.

'Penny for them,' Imogen said.

'Oh, sorry, I drifted away for a moment... I was thinking about you and James, how you make such a lovely couple. It would be a shame if it all... fell apart.'

'Yes, yes, it would. So I will not let such a stupid thing happen.' She sat up straight and lifted her shoulders. 'Enough of that shit. Now, tell me what happened with you and Tim.'

Now it was Julie's turn to shrug. Although she still thought about Tim, and about their break-up, nothing was yet clear to her. 'I don't know,' she said. 'It felt like he was drifting away from me.' Imo nodded, but whether in understanding or in encouragement wasn't clear. She would draw the story out, and sympathise; it was another thing at which she was adept. And perhaps it would be better, Julie thought, to talk to Imogen rather than Sarah, who knew Tim and his friends too well.

Julie lit a cigarette and breathed the smoke into the afternoon. She told Imogen everything. Imogen asked pertinent questions, sympathized, gave advice, and offered suggestions.

'Do you really want to get back together with him?' Imogen said.

Julie shook her head. 'I don't know. He's not the only fish in the sea.'

Imogen looked at Julie, her head tilted to one side, an eyebrow raised. 'I hear you've already been fishing.'

'What?' Julie said, although she knew what Imogen meant.

'Mark saw you in Gray's car with Chris and Simon. He said you and Si looked cosy.'

Julie knew she was smiling, although she had instead wanted to look mysterious. 'I do like Simon.'

'Well, everybody likes Simon,' Imogen said. 'Simon, Stuart and James were always my favourites. But Simon is a bit... backward at coming forward, isn't he?'

'He's shy,' Julie said. 'He doesn't know how to jump the first hurdle.'

'If he only realised how few hurdles he needs to jump.'

'And how some of us have no hurdles at all.'

They both giggled.

'That sounds terrible,' Julie said. 'So, let's just say then, in Simon's case, many of us would happily trim our hurdles.'

'No more!' Imogen laughed. 'I don't wish to know what you've been trimming.'

They both looked out of the window, into the street and across the hot grey pavements, where young people passed by in light summer dresses, jeans, tee-shirts, sandals, and shorts. Julie stretched. She was happy here, spending time with Imo. She realised how much she'd missed this group of friends. How different her world had become by going out with Tim.

'Still, you have a choice of boyfriends.' Julie said. 'Some of us simply can't afford to be so picky.'

Imogen laughed, a musical tinkling, and then squeezed Julie's hand. 'Oh, don't be silly. Look at you. You're gorgeous! I wish I had hair like yours, and those lovely blue eyes. You always seem to be smiling, and that smile comes out through those eyes.'

Julie loved Imogen at that moment for her laugh, and the squeeze of her hand, for saying the right things. But even being told by a Pre-Raphaelite beauty that you too were gorgeous wasn't enough when each day every mirror presented contrary evidence.

'What's happening with the others?' Julie said. 'I mean, I see Stu, Charlie, and Kate in town, but I don't get to talk to them as much as I did when I hung out here.'

'Well, Stuart and Kate are together.'

Julie nodded. 'Yes, I've seen them walking around looking snuggly. That's kind of fab, isn't it?'

'It is. And it removes temptation.'

'What?'

Imogen laughed. 'Well, you know, things haven't been going well with James, and Stuart and I have always been close. Sometimes, it's hard to resist. Sometimes I think things might be a little more stable with him.'

Imo had a soft spot for Stu. Julie knew that. Everybody knew that. Nobody made a big deal about it. Imo and Stu hugged and flirted, gave each other friendly kisses, and went places together. Imo and Stu had been that way with each other for years. They had almost been a couple; there had been some dates, some kissing. Then James had made a play for her. James and Stuart were best friends, and Stuart had been cool about it. James was relaxed with how close Stu and Imo remained. It was all very grown-up.

After a moment, Imogen continued. 'Charlie, however, has been weird.' She bit her lip.'

'He often could be.'

If anybody was bothered by Stuart and Imogen's closeness, it was Charlie. He was tall, skinny, sarcastic, funny, but there was something a little gothic about him; something of the night. Julie found it hard to believe Charlie enjoyed the languidness and light of this hot long summer.

'He's become most obsessed with Stuart,' Imogen said. 'He thinks Stu is going to... Well, to have sex with me.'

'Well, you did just say it was a possibility, ' Julie said.

'Ah, yes. Well, that's a passing fancy, unlikely to happen. Charlie thinks it *will* happen.'

'So why does that matter? I mean... Oh. Of course.' Julie's

comment tailed off. Because if everybody knew Imogen and Stuart were close, everybody also knew that Charlie had been obsessed with Imogen. He had felt himself in competition with Stuart to win her over. Charlie still competed, even though Stu and Imo were only friends now, even though Imo was with James.

'But Charlie does have a girlfriend now,' Imogen said. 'So I hope he'll forget all that nonsense.'

Julie had sometimes thought Charlie so intense and sarcastic that finding a girlfriend would be next to impossible. 'He does? Who?'

'You know Paul, in Devon?' Julie nodded. 'Well, Paul has a sister, Jane. She's sixteen now, and always thought Charlie was... *intriguing*. Last time Charlie was down at Paul's, things happened between him and Jane.'

'Oh. Well, that's good for Charlie, then.' Julie looked across the table. 'Good for you, too. Good for Stuart.'

'Yes, hurrah indeed. About time.'

'What's young Jane like? I must surely have seen her when they lived here?

'Well, she's older now, of course. A proper grown-up young lady. Old enough for the likes of Charles. Stuart says she's pretty. A bit of a smooth. Amusing. Really into flying saucers. She can't wait to visit here.'

Dereham was at the centre of a flying saucer flap, and had been for more than five years now. The town attracted skywatchers and ufologists from all over. The Dereham mystery had been discussed in books and even on local television programmes. There might be something to it all, Julie supposed, though she hadn't really given it too much thought. She knew Imogen and her friends were interested, but sceptical. And Charlie was the biggest sceptic of them all. 'So will Charlie become a skywatcher now?'

'Well, love does strange things to people.' Imogen laughed then, quietly. 'I mean, look at me, still hanging around with the beardy weirdy. All I know is what Stu tells me. Jane is crazy about these things, and wants to visit Copsehill with Charlie so they can skywatch together.'

'Oh my,' Julie said. 'Let's hope he doesn't get as obsessed with UFOs as he got with... *you*.'

'I bloody hope not.' Imogen sighed. 'That way lies madness.' She finished her drink. 'I suppose I'd better go and see what James is up to.'

Julie finished her drink as well. 'I don't know what I'm doing for the rest of the afternoon. Wandering around I suppose.'

'Oh! Do you want to come with me? '

Julie shook her head. 'That wasn't a hint.'

'Well, I didn't think was. But you'd be welcome at James's.'

'Thanks for the offer,' Julie said. 'But I'll wander around town and see what excitement I find.'

Imogen stood then. She wore frayed denim shorts that had been hidden by the table at which they sat. Her long legs were lightly tanned. She pulled on her stripy blazer. In this summer of relentless heat, horses would sweat, Julie thought, she would perspire, but Imo, in her blazer, would only glow. Imogen put on her sunglasses. Aviator shades, denim shorts, and her trusty stripy blazer – she could hardly look more glamorous. She and Julie left together. Imogen put an arm around Julie's shoulders. 'It's been good to see you,' she said. 'You should come and see us more often. Even if you get back with Tim.'

'I'll try,' Julie said. She narrowed her eyes as she left the darkness of the pub and walked into the bright, hot, afternoon sunlight.

'Oh, look,' Imogen said, quietly. 'We've already found all the excitement the town can offer.'

Julie looked down the road, and saw Simon and Stuart there, coming towards them. Simon smiled at her.

'I'll take Stuart,' Imogen said. 'And you can have Simon. Deal?'

'Well, of course it is,' Julie said. 'There's nothing wrong with Stu, of course, but I'd rather have young Simon.'

'Stuart does look good, doesn't he?'

Julie thought Imogen sounded perhaps a little too interested. Still, she did put up with James's habits and excesses, and had once fancied Stuart. Julie couldn't help wondering if something had happened, or would happen, between them. Imogen skipped down the steps, smiling, towards Stuart, her long hair curling over her shoulders. She gave him a hug.

'Bye, Julie,' Imogen said. 'It was good to see you!' She and Stuart headed across the car park, and then crossed the road, walking quickly towards Church Street. Julie said hello to Simon, but watched Imogen talking animatedly to Stuart.

'Is anything going on with those two?' Julie said.

Simon shrugged. 'No idea.'

'Where are you off to?'

'To the park. Nick and Mark should be there by now.'

'Mark went to James's.'

'Well, he's supposed to be meeting me and Nick near the swings at two.'

Julie glanced at her watch. It was just coming up to two o'clock. 'So, what do you plan to do there?'

'There is no *plan*. It's just a place to meet up that isn't a pub. Nick hasn't got much money. Neither have I, come to that. We might have a go on the putting green. Perhaps laze around. Perhaps we might walk somewhere else. Although I'm a bit knackered.'

Julie and Simon walked out of the Market Place towards the park. 'Where did you walk to?' Julie said.

'Red Post Hill, over the ridge to Copsehill, and then back round the Tump to Derebury. It was bloody hot. The ground is rock hard. And dusty. There was a nice breeze on top of Copsehill, though.'

'Wish I'd gone with you,' Julie said. 'I miss that walk.' She hadn't walked much – hardly at all, in fact – with Tim. He had a car, and didn't see much point in walking now. She should walk more, she decided. She could walk by herself. And really, even if she did get back together with Tim, what was to stop her going for a walk with Simon and Stuart? Or just Simon for that matter. It's not as if she and Tim were married.

The sun was at its zenith, and the afternoon already hot. The wind hardly moved. Julie's arms were bare, and she felt the sun already burning her pale skin. They talked about Simon's long walk with Stuart; the hills and the views, the paths, the heat, and the bright sun. They talked about Stuart, and James, and about Mark and Honeyhouse.

Interesting though all this was, there was only one thing Julie currently needed to know. 'So tell me, Simon. Are Stuart and Imo doing it?' she said. 'Did he say anything at all?'

'But... but...' Simon spluttered. 'Imo and James are back together, aren't they?'

'Yes. However, Imo and Stu have always been close, you know that. And Imo and James have had a few problems. They did break up for a little while. So who knows what might have happened.'

'Well, you were with Imo just now. Did she say anything to you?'

'Nothing, but then girls are more discreet than boys. Boys do so like to boast.'

'And girls do like to gossip.'

'That's rather a sweeping statement.'

'So was yours.'

Julie laughed. 'Yeah, right.' She walked beside Simon on the path by the dry, wilting flowerbeds. They passed quietly through the gates and into the park. Julie tried again. 'Do you know *anything*?'

'Do *you*?'

'Are you asking me that because you *do* know something, and want some repayment in kind?'

'I'm wondering if Imo told *you* something that you're now asking me to confirm.'

'No. There were subtle hints, perhaps. There was something playful about her that was, you know... *challenging,* as if she wanted me to ask.'

34

'Oh no. You're not going to start wittering about intuition.'

'I might.'

'You know Stu and Kate are together?'

'Yes,' Julie said.

'And Kate is Imogen's best friend. Would Kate go out with Stu if she knew that there'd been shenanigans?' Simon paused doubtfully. 'Would she?'

Well, 'I suppose not.' Julie sighed theatrically. 'But is it wrong of me to want shenanigans?'

'Depends on who you want them with.'

Julie looked at Simon and raised an eyebrow. 'I mean between them.'

'It would undoubtedly be news. Good gossip. The Lion would be simply agog. The world would shift on its axis. Charlie would freak.' Simon paused. 'Stu and Imo, eh? Much as I like the pair of them, it would be so very wrong.'

They found Nick and Mark sitting near a large and spreading chestnut tree. Swings and roundabouts were close by. A paddling pool, full of water, looked clean and invitingly cool. There were no children in the park. Schools had yet to break for summer. Only the college boys and girls were out to play this afternoon. Julie and Simon sat beneath the heavy branches of the tree.

Julie turned to Simon, and winked. 'Under the spreading chestnut tree, I'll kiss you and you'll kiss me.'

'Really?' Simon said. 'Seems a bit extravagant for a hot day.'

Simon, Nick and Mark caught up with each other's news. Julie wondered if Mark knew anything about Imo and Stu, but decided not to ask. She leaned back against the tall old tree, next to Simon. Nick was lying on the burnt grass, his eyes closed. Mark sat beside him, in the sun, his legs out in front of him, leaning backwards slightly, his weight on his hands behind him, his face turned up to the blue sky.

'I'm getting a headache,' Mark said. 'The sun is just so... *bloody* hot.'

'You need to be in the shade, then,' Julie said. 'You might get sunstroke. You too, Nick. Come on over here.'

'Yes, mum,' Mark said. He shuffled back into the shade beneath the tree. The wind was at its lightest now and the dry leaves rattled softly.

Despite Julie's concern, Nick stayed exactly where he was. He appeared almost impervious to heat. He still had on his black tee-shirt. He was tanned, though – his arms and face were brown. 'I love all this sun,' he mumbled.

The gate from the footpath opened and two girls entered the play park. One was blonde and tall, the other dark, shorter, about Julie's height. Julie knew who the blonde girl was – Heather, from Southleigh. She guessed, then, that the dark-haired girl also came from there. She wondered what had brought them here. Hardly Dereham itself. There was, after all, very little to choose between Dereham and Southleigh. Both were small market towns losing identity as connections to agriculture fell away. Both towns lacked amenities. But buses ran between the towns. Why not, thought Julie, travel while you had the opportunity? She and Simon had, after all, joined in the whimsical jaunt to Stonehenge and Beacon Hill just yesterday. And this summer, this long drowsing dream of a summer, would be over far too soon.

'Well, hello,' said Mark, his voice low. 'And who would those young ladies be?'

'The blonde is Heather,' Julie said. 'She sometimes comes into The Swan. She went out with that guy Hobo. You know him, don't you?' Mark nodded. 'But that ended a few months back. I haven't seen her since.'

The girls made their way to the swings. Heather's friend sat on one of them. Heather leaned against the bright red cast-iron supporting framework. She wore bell-bottom jeans, black daps, and a white tee-shirt that she had knotted tight above her navel. But most extraordinarily, given the heat, she also wore a long, red, velvet dressing gown. That the gown had once belonged to a man was obvious; it fell to the ground like a duster.

36

Julie didn't know Heather well. She had of course slyly watched her, and watched men watching her, in The Swan. Heather was very confident. She had wide grey eyes in a tanned oval face, and sensual lips. She had always seemed friendly. She had said hello to Julie in The Swan, had passed some time with her when they had both been standing at the bar. Julie had no cause to dislike Heather, apart from the blonde hair – that was, of course, somehow more perfect than hers – and the lips, and the self-esteem.

Nick sat up, piqued by Mark's words. He looked across towards the swings. Heather looked across at him, and then away. She lit two cigarettes, handed one to her dark-haired friend who swung slowly in small arcs, pushing herself with a black baseball boot, slowly, somnolently. She looked at the ground, smoking. She was indifferent to everyone and everything: to Heather, and to Nick and Mark; to the park, to the dazzling sun, to the heat and to the blue sky. Her shag cut hair was dyed pitch black.

Heather began to sing. *I'm counting out time*, she sang, and clicked her fingers. *Hoping it goes like I planned it*. Her friend smiled, then. *Cos I understand it*, Heather sang. Damn her, Julie thought, she can sing as well. Julie recognised Heather's song. She didn't know it well, but she'd heard it played often enough on record players this past year. Heather still softly sang and clicked her fingers to the beat, swinging her hips slowly from side to side. Her long dressing gown swept dust from the sun-baked ground and brown grass. Julie knew that Heather was flirting with the boys, and flirting in ways that Julie knew she could not. Did she wish she could? She wasn't sure. And yet, to have such confidence...

Nick stood up. Mark also stood then. They walked across to the swings.

'I foresee courting,' Simon said. 'Wooing. A dalliance, perchance.'

Mark sat in the swing next to Heather's friend. Nick stood next to Heather. Mark offered the girls cigarettes.

'Heather isn't backward at coming forwards,' Julie said, frowning.

Simon shrugged. 'So, she likes to sing and dance. There's nothing wrong with that.'

'But must she be quite so... *brazen?*'

Simon laughed gently now. 'Oh, Jules. It was hardly *brazen*, was it?'

'But she *was* showing herself off.' Heather's blonde hair glittered in the afternoon sun, goading Julie. 'Mark and Nick were over there like rats up a drainpipe. Look at them.' She plucked at the dry grass around her. 'She's not even that attractive.'

Simon was looking at the swings. 'This is the first time I've seen her. But I must say... objectively... that she *is* rather good looking.' He looked at Julie now with a slightly bewildered air. He couldn't know from what motive Julie had said what she had said; but Simon's response had been both what she'd wanted him to say, and not wanted him to say. Saying it gave her the opportunity to vent some frustration.

She sighed. 'You're all the same. Long legs, fine, firm young breasts, a pretty face and you're all over it, aren't you.' She felt the need to goad Simon. She didn't really know why she was doing this. 'Don't you want to go over there and join them?'

Simon looked at her, his eyebrows drawn down. 'Well, I'd rather be here with you.'

The momentarily intense conflict within Julie faded. 'I won't mind if you go over.'

'Oh, don't be ridiculous, Jules,' Simon said, softly. 'I'm happy to carry on sitting with you.'

Julie relaxed then, her head now on Simon's shoulder. She wasn't sure what she was doing with him. She was still confused about Tim, and she knew Simon was also confused. She didn't know why Heather had so disturbed her. Perhaps it was because Heather was so comfortable in herself, so in control of what she did. Julie, meanwhile, knew that she was herself flirting with

Simon, and possibly out of control, with no idea where she was heading. Of course, she had always liked Simon - but it was only when she saw him yesterday afternoon that she had a desire... no, a *need* to move in closer to Simon. She had felt an eagerness to be touched.

Julie took Simon's arm, put it around her, and made herself more comfortable on his shoulder. She watched Mark and Nick talking to Heather and the other girl. There were smiles over there, laughter. They'd already separated into couples. Nick and Heather, the other girl and Mark. Would Mark do anything with this girl, though? Everybody knew he only wanted Chrissie. Julie found herself now rooting for Heather's friend. Anything that night break Mark's enthrallment to the wispy Chrissie would be welcome.

'What about this girl you like, Si? Anna? What's happening with her?'

'I have *no* idea,' Simon said. 'She's somewhere in a village near Southleigh. That's all I know right now.'

'What's she like?'

Simon told the tale. The flirting. The laughing and liking. The leaving. The story was just a little sad, a little hopeless, filled with pathos. And yet it was also romantic, and the way Simon told it filled Julie with a warmth, an innocent longing of her own, a desire to see some kind of completion for him. 'She sounds great,' Julie said, smiling. She meant it. Anna did sound great, the kind of girl who – if Simon could ever get past the hurdles of his own insecurity, his lack of belief in himself, and his lack of experience – would make a fine girlfriend for him. At the same time, the story, and the way he told it, made her want to hug Simon close to her and offer him comfort.

Nick sauntered back, and knelt down in front of Julie and Simon. 'Hello there. Heather and Mary want to go to the putting green. Do you want to come with us?'

Julie had no desire to go. She glanced at Simon, wondering if he would want to go with them. There was perhaps adventure there.

Simon shook his head. 'We'll be fine. You go off and do some flirting.'

'We'll be down the Lion later, anyway, I should think,' Nick said. He returned to Heather, and then the four of them headed towards the putting green. Heather looked over. She waved at Julie and Simon. Julie returned the wave.

'Shall we walk somewhere?' Simon said.

'Oh, yes, let's do that,' Julie said.

They stood and dusted themselves down. As they walked out of the gate, and onto the path that led around the park, Julie took Simon's hand. She wasn't entirely sure why.

3

This is Above

Thin clouds of blue and grey laced the orange haze at the end of another hot day. The unmoving air was so thick and so humid even the birds refused to sing. Yesterday, out on the downs, there had been at least a breeze, Simon recalled fondly. Here in town the evening was still, sultry. He felt it should thunder, although a storm had yet to punctuate the long hot days of this always sweltering summer. Simon had walked up Magpie Road from home, and now turned right onto Goldfinch Drive. He looked over towards Gray's house, and was unsurprised to see Gray and Chris leaning against the wing of the Vitesse. The bonnet of the black car was open. Any plans they were hatching could hardly involve a long drive into the warm night. As Simon approached them, Chris nodded. 'Simon! Where are you off to this evening?'

'The White Lion, of course.'

Gray looked at Chris. 'We should go with him, get ourselves a drink.'

Chris nodded, and then lit a cigarette, blew the grey smoke into the hazy sky. Chris's hands were covered in oil and grease. 'Yes, we should,' Chris said. 'It's been quite a day.'

Simon walked to the front of the Vitesse, and looked under the open bonnet. Hoses dangled, and electrical wires hung loose; the battery, alternator, radiator and carburettors had all been removed. The engine bay contained only a stripped straight six, covered in oil. 'Well, you don't hang around, do you' Simon said.

Chris took a long drag on his cigarette, then he turned and leaned on the Vitesse's wing. He also peered into the engine bay. 'That noise, remember? I reckon it's a piston ring. Need to change the bastard thing.'

'Long job,' Simon said. He'd many times watched his old man strip a greasy engine down.

'Well, we'll do it in a couple of days. We'll lift the engine out tomorrow.'

Gray smiled then. 'When he says *we*, that does *not* include me. I'm only making coffee. He'll have to find some other helpful souls.'

'So what do you need help with?' Simon asked.

'Some lifting,' Chris said.

'I'll help,' Simon said. He had nothing else to do until the summer ended and autumn came around, only his Sunday morning paper-round. He wondered if he was the oldest paper-boy in Dereham, if not the whole of Wilshire.

'Good man,' Gray said. 'I'll make *you* coffee, too.'

'You're *very* kind,' Simon said.

'Yes, I *am*.'

42

Chris looked at his hands. 'These need to be cleaned.'

'Well, do get on with it, young man,' Gray huffed. 'I'm bloody desperate to get a drink.'

Chris threw his dying cigarette into a flower bed where it landed between drooping marigolds and a cosmos, and then walked down the path beside the house to the door that took him into the kitchen.

'Someone was looking for you earlier,' Gray said to Simon. 'A young blonde floozy.'

It could only be Julie, Simon thought. 'Julie?' he said. 'What could she want with me?'

'You, of course. I met her this afternoon. Despite seeing you only yesterday, she was nonetheless wondering if we – and by *we*, I think she meant *you*, of course – were going to the pub tonight.'

'Well, of course we're going to the pub tonight. Did she say why she was looking for me?'

'She *wants* you,' Gray said, drawing out the verb.

'Very amusing,' Simon said. 'Most droll.'

Gray round face broke into a grin. 'She didn't say, actually. Played her cards very close to her fine chest. Secretive you could say. Even, perhaps, a little sly. She's a minx, that's what she is.'

Chris walked back up the path with another cigarette burning between his lips. 'Are we going to the Lion, or what?'

'Of course we are,' Gray said. 'Let's get going.'

Chris dropped the bonnet of the Vitesse. 'Right, Gray, get a move on, lock up the house.'

Gray moved towards the house, but after a few steps stopped and stared sadly at his car. 'I miss her,' he said. He looked down Goldfinch Drive. 'And we have to walk all the way to the pub.'

'It's not *that* far,' Simon said. 'You baby.'

'Not for you, but you *are* a kung fu master.'

Simon sighed and feigned modesty. 'Well, yes, I suppose I bloody well am.'

'Oh, do get on with it, Gray,' Chris pleaded. 'I'm absolutely desperate for a pint.'

Gray turned towards the house, but stopped again and frowned at the Vitesse. 'But we're young, and free, and single...' Gray said. 'We have endless sunny days and no car... It's just not right. It makes me very sad.'

Chris sucked on his cigarette and looked at the garage door. 'Shame your Mum took the keys to the Mini,' Chris said. 'We could take that.'

Simon and Gray also regarded the door, as if the answer to an unasked question lurked behind it. Simon then looked at Chris. 'I would've thought with your mechanical nous you could start a Mini with no key.'

Chris looked at Simon, then the garage door. He threw his cigarette end into the flower bed again. This time the burning butt landed between what looked like a daisy, and what Simon believed his mother called a nasturtium – although flowers remained, in general, a mystery to him. Simon rather liked the way his friend Gaz categorised flowers – whatever the season, if it was blue it was a tulip, if yellow it was a daffodil, if red, a rose, if white, of course, a daisy.

'I can do that,' Chris said. 'I can hot-wire a car.'

'You can do that?' Gray said.

'I said I can.'

'Well, get on it with then my good fellow. There are drinks to be drunk, drives to be.... druv.'

'What about the garage door?'

'What about it?'

'It's locked. Your mum took the key to that. too.'

'Why, it's almost as if,' Simon said, 'your mum foresaw such a situation.'

Gray laughed. 'Damn and blast all parents,' he said. 'They like to think they know everything.'

Simon nodded. 'They do seem most prescient.'

They all turned to look at the garage door and examined it most thoughtfully. Finally, Simon said, 'If your door is anything like the one at our house, the lock only stops the handle turning.'

Gray frowned. 'That is the function of a lock.'

'Have you ever looked at how the handle actually works?' Simon asked.

'Of course not,' Gray said. I have much better things to do.'

'When you twist the handle, it pulls wires at the back of the door. The wires pull the... uh, metal bits that go into rebates.'

'The deadbolts,' Chris said.

'Yeah, right, the deadbolts. If you go into the garage and pull the cords, you can open the door.'

Gray opened his eyes wide. 'Can we do that?'

'Oh! Yes, we *can* do that!' Chris said. 'Simon, that is two brilliant ideas in one day. If Julie were here I'd ask her to kiss you twice, once for each outstanding idea.'

'Just buy me an orange juice instead,' Simon said.

Chris and Gray walked down the path and then through the side door that led into the garage. A few moments later the door slowly rose. 'We have lift-off!' Gray said triumphantly. He looked at the green Mini, his eyes bright. 'Think of the endless possibilities now we have access to a car again.'

Simon idly wondered if Gray was insured to drive his mum's car. He thought it better not to ask. Some things were not worth knowing.

Chris went to the front of the Mini and lifted the bonnet. Simon opened the driver's side door. Gray's mother had, then, not thought of everything that might go wrong. Chris's voice came from under the bonnet. 'Alright, Gray. Make sure it's out of gear.'

Gray leaned into the car and shook the gear stick. 'Any time you're ready to go,' he said.

Simon heard sparks, the starter motor sang, the car lurched forward, and Chris jumped backwards, banging his head on the bonnet. Gray laughed. Simon winced. Chris looked ruefully over the bonnet, rubbing the back of his head and frowning. 'That gearbox is getting bit a sloppy,' Chris remarked. 'This time, Gray, get in the car, push the clutch in, put the gear stick in first, then second, and *then* put it into neutral.'

Gray did as he was told. Sparks flew again, the starter motor turned, and the engine coughed, sputtered and then chattered into life.

'Excellent,' Gray said. 'To the Lion we go!'

Gray reversed the Mini past the Vitesse and into the road. Chris closed the garage door. Simon climbed into the back of the Mini, and Chris jumped into the passenger seat. 'This is already an adventure,' Gray said.

They sped down Goldfinch Drive to the crossroads with Barton Road. Gray turned left, into town.

Chris looked at Gray. 'Did you lock the back door?'

'Oh, shit. No.'

'So we should go back,' Chris said.

'Man, you're grown up,' Gray said. 'Are you my dad? There's no time to turn back. And anyway, Dereham's hardly a hotbed of crime.'

Simon supposed it unnecessary to mention that the Wright's, at the bottom of Magpie Road, had been burgled last week. He knew that Gray would never turn back now.

They arrived in town. Gray pulled up next to the pavement just down from the Market Place, deliberately stalling the Mini just as Chris had instructed him to do. Gray could have parked up in the Market Place, much closer to the doors of the White Lion, but that would require unnecessary manoeuvring, which Gray liked to avoid. Simon looked out of his window at the distance from the Mini to the pavement. It was not the best of Gray's achievements. Headlights lit up the inside of the car as another vehicle pulled up behind. Gray exited the car, and headed straight for the pub, leaving Chris to lift the bonnet and undo the magic that made the car go. Chris let the bonnet drop and close itself, and then he and Simon followed Gray into the pub. The car that had parked behind the Mini was an army Land Rover. The driver and passenger wore the red caps of the military police. Dereham wasn't an army town, like Tidworth or Bulford, but squaddies came into town for a drink. For them it made a pleasant change from the tedium of the garrisons in which they were stationed. At least, Simon thought, the MPs could watch over the unlocked Mini.

Gray had already bought Simon an orange juice and Chris a pint of 6X. They turned and looked around the crowded bar that was full of smoke and people talking. Bryan Ferry warbled from the jukebox. *Let's Stick Together*, he suggested. Simon pointed to a small brown table next to where his friend Mark was sitting. Simon, Gray and Chris squeezed around the table, and said hello to Mark. Simon glanced at the tables near him, and then looked around the saloon bar. He discerned the ever-overlapping Venn diagram of social acquaintance. Mark was sitting with Simon's other friends Gaz and Nick. Mark had positioned himself so that he could also talk to Danny, Steve and John, members of Honeyhouse, the band in which Mark played bass and guitar. When this group of friends all sat together, people would invariably refer to them as, of course, the Honeyhouse gang. Next to their table was the group of friends jokingly referred to as the Prophets, as they all had beards, long and scruffy hair, and questionable sartorial nous: Charlie, tall, faintly gothic; elfin James; and Stuart, the badminton-playing one. With them sat the girls, Kate and Imogen. James wrote lyrics for Honeyhouse, so the Prophets had arranged themselves so that James could also talk to the Honeyhouse gang. When Simon, Gray and Chris had sat at the table next to Mark, they arranged themselves so that Simon could talk to Mark, as well as to Stuart on the Prophets' table. Gray, meanwhile, placed himself such that he could flirt with Chrissie, with whom Mark also flirted. Jake, Chrissie's boyfriend, was a mechanic, thus inevitably ended up sitting near Chris, and, as it happened, they had mechanical things to discuss. And so it continued. Simon could trace friendships, acquaintanceships and courtships that spiralled and overlapped and intersected all around the blue-clouded, noisy bar.

The door opened, and Simon looked over. Julie came in. She looked across at Simon and smiled and waved. Simon returned the wave. Julie bought herself a drink, and then came over and sat with him and Chris and Gray.

'How are you?' Simon said. 'Good to see you.'

Julie sipped her drink. Her blue eyes were bright over the top of her glass. 'I'm good.'

'I hear you were looking for me.'

'I was.'

'Any reason?'

'I wanted to make sure you'd be here tonight. To charm and amuse me, naturally.'

'Are you sure you were looking for me, then?'

'And you did say I should return to my old watering hole.'

'You should,' Mark said. 'We miss you. Why you would want to frequent The Swan is beyond me.'

'Well, you know,' Julie said quietly. 'Tim likes it there... and... well, we were...' She shrugged.

'You don't need him,' Gray said. 'How do you feel about him now? Are you okay with it?'

'Yes, I'm okay about it,' Julie said.

Simon wondered whether she really was. When she had entered the bar and sat down with them she had been happy, smiling, and the light and the life that could so often brighten her eyes had been dancing in them. For a brief moment, though, after she had mentioned Tim, she had seemed confused, less sure, and the light in her eyes had faded.

Julie nodded towards Nick. 'So,' she said to Simon, 'he escaped the clutches of the lovely Heather.'

'Barely,' Simon said.' He has a date with her tomorrow, over in Southleigh.'

'The other girl? Mary?'

'Mark's not interested.'

'What is much more interesting,' Gray said, interrupting them, 'is that we now have a car if you fancy a trip somewhere.

48

You name a place, and I'll drive you right there. As long as you pay for the petrol.'

Julie raised an eyebrow. 'Chris fixed the car?'

'Not so much,' Chris said. 'We have his mum's car.'

'How the... No, don't answer that. I don't think I want to know *how*.'

Chris lit a cigarette, looked at Simon. 'It was his idea, really. Clever boy.' Chris laughed and tapped some ash into a tray.

'Well, I only provided suggestions.'

'And most welcome they were, too' Gray said.

Simon shook his head. 'You know, it wasn't *actually* my idea to steal your mum's car.'

Gray shrugged. 'Can I steal from my own family? I'm sure my mother would have happily lent me the car, had she been here to ask.'

Simon shook his head. 'I'm not so sure about that?'

'Well, okay, perhaps not *happily*.'

'Oh, yes! Of course!' Chris said. He looked at Julie. 'I'm glad you've arrived. I can save myself a pretty penny. I said to Simon earlier that you should give him a kiss for each of his brilliant suggestions. But you weren't there, so he demanded drinks. But now you *are* here, so, if you'd oblige...'

Julie turned and looked into Simon's eyes; he was pleased to see the twinkle back in hers. She leaned across the table and kissed him, first on one cheek, and then on the other. Each kiss was light, slow, and her cheek felt soft; between each kiss she paused to look at him with a soft, beguiling, cheeky smile.

'Thanks,' Chris said.

Julie's smile was wide now. 'Oh, you still owe him drinks. I did that for my benefit.'

'You can't do-' Chris's complaint was cut off by the sudden wail of the siren that called firemen to the station in White Street. The siren was drowned out by the jukebox which had started playing *Devil Woman*.

49

Danny, at the Honeyhouse table, abruptly scraped his chair back and stood up. 'Who the hell put this shit on!' he shouted. He glared around the bar. There was laughing, but nobody answered. Simon noticed, though, that Chrissie looked a little shifty.

'Enough of that shit,' James said. 'It's a fine song.'

James might well think it a fine song, Simon thought. James was nothing if not eclectic.

'You should write lyrics like that,' Danny said. 'Oh, *she's just a devil woman*,' he sang. He sat down. 'It would make a pleasant change from all that hippie shit you write for us.'

'You only say that,' James replied, 'because my hippie shit has words of more than two syllables and you can't pronounce them.'

Danny laughed. 'Piss off, you pretentious hippie.'

Simon shook his head, and chuckled. 'I'm guessing,' he said quietly to Julie, 'that James and Danny have already had a few.'

Julie nodded. 'A joint or two, as well. I think Danny was with James earlier, writing some songs. So, I guess there'd be a few glasses of Martell, some grass, then down the pub.'

'It's no wonder Imogen's frowning.'

Julie looked around, and leaned in closer. 'James is a fool,' she said, sotto voce. 'She told him he must slow down his drinking.' She paused. 'And then, of course, there's Stuart.' She looked questioningly at Simon.

'What about him?' Simon said. 'What's happened?'

'You know,' Julie said. She nodded slowly, encouragingly, and then winked at Simon. 'What I said yesterday... Do you remember?'

Simon looked at Stuart, and then at Kate. 'Well, no. I don't actually remember.'

'Yeah. Well, I'm just guessing, but I think that–'

What Julie had guessed was interrupted by Chris standing up. 'What *is* that?' he said. The rising and falling of a siren cut over the outro to *Devil Woman*. 'It seems to be coming very close to us.'

Chris went over to a hazy window. Blue flashing lights lit his wiry fair hair. He half-turned, and addressing himself to the gaggle of people behind him, said 'It's only a police car. It's stopped across the middle of the road. Like... a road block.' He paused. 'The police are stopping traffic...'

The chugalug rhythm of *I Love to Boogie* started up from the jukebox.

'Now that's more like it,' Danny said to James.

'Right on,' James replied, raising his glass.

'The coppers are looking towards the shops.' Chris said. He had to speak more loudly now; everybody was talking to each other about what was happening on the street outside. 'I wonder if the bookshop's burning,' Chris said.

There was the sound of another siren. Blue light strobed across the walls of the town before the vehicle even came into view. 'Here comes the fire engine,' Chris reported. 'It's slowing.... it's stopped. By the police car. And there's another police car coming.

'Let's go and look,' Julie said.

She and Simon went outside, and stood at the top of the steps by the front of the White Lion with a few others who drank and observed all the excitement.

'You're nosy,' Simon said.

'Inquisitive,' Julie said. She looked around eagerly.

A fireman exited the fire engine and followed a policeman across the road. They met two military policemen. They began to examine the Mini.

'Shit,' Simon said. 'That's Gray's car. What the hell...'

Simon ran back inside, where he met Chris on the way out. 'It's Gray's car,' Simon said.

Chris looked around vaguely, and then said, 'Christ, Gray's car!' He ran back inside the pub to find Gray.

Simon returned to Julie. They watched as a fireman opened

the unlocked driver's door to the Mini, and then looked around the steering wheel, the footwell and dashboard. The policeman tried to open the boot. Unlike the doors, that had remained locked.

Gray ran out of the pub. 'Make way,' he shouted, pushing between Simon and Julie. Chris hurried after Gray. James, Imogen, Mark, Nick, Danny, and others followed, carrying their glasses. The night was warm. The Market Place had taken on the atmosphere of a party. Blue and amber lights flashed and reflected back from the windows and doors of the shops, like a gigantic disco mirror ball. Music flowed through the open windows of pubs. People laughed and chatted, and smoked and danced. Further down the road, on the other side of the road-block, people had come out of The Swan and The Rising Sun to observe. Mark offered a cigarette to Julie. James lit a black Sobranie, sipped at his brandy. 'This is why I don't drive,' he said.

'You don't drive because you can't,' Imogen said.

A fireman lifted the Mini's bonnet. Julie took Simon's hand, and pulled him down the steps. 'Let's get closer,' she said. 'This could be a laugh.'

Simon playfully restrained Julie, but then allowed himself to be led down the steps to the pavement. 'I do believe I said you were nosy.'

'Yes,' Julie said. 'And as I pointed out, I am merely a little inquisitive.'

They stopped a short distance from the Mini, and leaned against a cool masonry wall. They could hear most of what was being said. A fireman talked to Gray and Chris. 'I need your car keys,' the fireman said. 'The battery is in the boot, and it's locked.'

Gray looked discombobulated, worried. He handed over a set of car keys while looking at police- and firemen. 'These should do it,' Gray said nervously.

The fireman tried first one, and then another key. Neither worked. Gray looked at the fireman then, as if suddenly aware of what had happened, and said, 'Oh, sorry, those will never work, they aren't the keys for this car, not at all.'

The fireman looked at the keys, then at Gray. 'So where are the keys? Are they in the pub?'

'I don't have them.'

'Not even in the bar?'

'No. My mum has them. She's on holiday.'

'So how did you start it?'

'By hotwiring it.'

The fireman laughed. 'Well, then. I'll just have to enter the boot another way.' He opened the passenger door, tilted the seat forward, and then pulled at the back of the rear seat.

Gray looked at Chris. There was confusion on his face. 'What's he doing to the car?'

'He's trying to take the back seat out. He can get through there to the battery.'

A policeman asked Simon who owned the car. Simon pointed to Gray. 'He does. Well, when, I say–'

The policeman had already moved the few paces over to Gray. 'Is this your car?'

Gray turned to the policeman. 'Yes. Of course.'

'How many miles has it done?'

Gray looked confused, then impish. 'Why, do you want to buy it?'

Julie sniggered. Simon gently nudged her. 'Behave,' he whispered. 'He might arrest us.'

'Seriously, how many?' the policeman asked.

Gray leaned in the passenger door and looked at the big, black speedometer.

'No, don't look!' the policeman said sharply.

'Oh! I see!' Gray said playfully. 'It's a quiz!'

'No! I'm trying to confirm you own this car.'

A police sergeant moved away from the other fireman, and came over to Gray. 'You'd better come along with me, young man.'

'Why?' Gray said.

The sergeant gestured around him. 'Let's take a look, shall we? There's a fire engine, four firemen, two police cars, and two bobbies. You've created quite a rumpus tonight. I'm afraid you need to make a statement.' He led Gray to one of the police cars.

'Oh, what a shame,' Julie said. 'Now we can't hear what nonsense he's going to come out with.'

There was a shout from inside Gray's Mini. 'Success!' The fireman threw the back of the rear seat into the driver's seat, and then he disappeared as he reached into the boot.

A bobby was looking into the Mini, watching the fireman. Simon leaned over to him. 'So, what on earth kicked all this off? '

'The MPs in the Land Rover behind saw smoke, so they radioed for a fire engine. And they had seen one of your mates, Chris, I guess' – the bobby was local and knew their faces – 'messing about under the bonnet, and got worried there might be a bomb under there.'

'A bomb?' Julie exclaimed. 'How fanciful!'

'Well, you can't be too careful these days,' the policeman said, 'There's lots of squaddies in the area. They like this town. It's a nice change for them. The town would be an easy target.'

'Really?' Simon said.

'Oh yes. The MPs were all for calling up the bomb squad, but the sergeant noted that a bunch of Micks were hardly likely to leave a smoking car in front of an army Land Rover, and then head off into the White Lion, of all places, for a drink while it went off. I mean... *the White Lion*...' He shook his head.

Julie nodded. 'Oh yes. So very true.' Her face was serious, but Simon thought that she was most likely being facetious. The narrowed eyes of the policeman suggested he thought the same.

The sergeant returned with Gray. Chris joined them. 'So, sir, just to be absolutely clear... Your mother did *not* give you permission to take her car and set fire to it, is that what you're saying?' Gray nodded. The sergeant looked over toward the Mini. 'So, then, how are you going to move it now?'

Chris shrugged. 'I suppose we can't hotwire it...'

The sergeant turned and scowled at Chris. 'Quite right.'

Chris nodded slowly. 'So we'll have to tow it.'

'But you don't have any lights,' the sergeant said.

'I know a way to get the lights to work,' Chris said cannily. 'But it'll mean, well... shorting things out.'

The sergeant shook his head. 'Well, if you must. But be very careful. We wouldn't want a repeat performance.'

'Where will we get a tow rope and a tow?' Gray appeared flustered. The chat in the car with the sergeant must have been serious.

'What about Jake,' Julie said. 'He's here, and he always comes into town by car.'

'Right!' Chris said. 'Come on, Gray, let's get you sorted out.' They ran into the Lion.

'I suppose we should join the others,' Simon said, although he was reluctant to do so.

The police cars and fire engines pulled away. A small figure loped along the pavement. Simon recognised Greaser. He walked fast, but slowed when he saw Simon and Julie. He looked wired. 'You guys got any dope?'

'Oh, do come off it, Greaser,' Julie said. 'Have you ever seen me with any dope?'

'Yeah, yeah, right,' Greaser said. 'Sorry Jules, man.' He glanced at Julie. 'Tim was in The Swan,' he said. 'He was asking after you.'

'Well, he can bugger right off,' Julie said.

Greaser bounced on the balls of his feet and looked at Simon. 'So what about you, mate, Simon isn't it? You got something? What were all the pigs doing out here? Any speed or anything? Some dexies?'

'I'm not really into drugs.' Simon said.

'Aren't you into violence, then? 'Cos, you know, you got to take drugs for that, haven't you?'

'Err, no,' Simon said.

'Ya strange,' Greaser said. 'Ya oughta get... mmm... to suit ya hairlines...'

Simon, nonplussed by this concatenation of non sequiturs, could only mumble in reply. 'Right on, Greaser,' he said.

'Yeah, right on, man. And you too, Jules. You're cool. I'll tell Tim you were looking for him.'

Julie frowned. 'I am not looking for him.'

Greaser laughed. 'Oh yeah, that's right, man. Right on. He was looking for you. Of course he was. Right. Yeah. Well, I'll let you know. Gotta go. Gotta find me something to smoke. Or drop. I wonder if Jeff is in town tonight?'

'The best of luck in your quest,' Simon said.

'Thanks, man,' Greaser said. 'You're a gent, you know. You don't have any speed for sale do you?'

Julie shook her head. 'No, we don't, Greaser. You should head off home. You don't really need any more of anything tonight.'

'Yeah, Jules, You're right. I'll go. I'll tell Tim that you were looking for him. So I'll go now. And you Simon, you really are a gent.' Greaser wandered off along the Market Place, towards Town Road.

Julie took Simon's hand again. 'We'd better join the others. They'll think we're up to shenanigans otherwise.'

Simon liked the feel of Julie's hand in his.

Julie looked at the departing Greaser, a shade now in the shadows of the street. 'I have no idea where he's going,' Jules said. 'He lives the other side of town.'

James had polished off another brandy or two while Simon and Julie were outside. He was complaining about the shite playing on the jukebox, and inviting everybody back to his place. Like most of his friends, James still lived with his parents; but he had rooms in the attic that were almost a flat. An only child, James was given freedoms by doting parents unknown to his friends. His parents were most tolerant, not seeming to care if James rolled in late with his friends. Danny, Steve and John from

Honeyhouse would most likely go back to James's place, but Imogen was obviously chary. She often stayed at James's house, because she lived in Burnt Norton, but Simon felt that if she could avoid staying tonight, she would. She could always get a lift with somebody, or crash at Stu's.

Simon leaned over to Julie, spoke softly. 'Do you want to go to James's tonight?'

Julie also spoke quietly. 'Not really. Imo isn't happy with the idea, and if we don't go, the others might not.'

Simon nodded. 'They're all pretty pissed, now. And there's grass at James's. They'll only get worse.'

'Well, let's not give any encouragement. Things could get heavy if Imo goes back.'

At that moment, Kate looked over. She mouthed *Are you going?* Simon frowned, shook his head. He leaned over to Mark and Nick and asked if they were going. Mark said no, they were heading for his to play some canasta. Simon looked at Kate, pointed to Nick and Mark, and shook his head. Kate gave him a thumbs-up, then leaned over to Imogen and whispered in her ear. Imogen stood up then, and came to sit between Simon and Julie. She looked around the table. 'So you're not going?'

'Oh, no,' Simon said.

'Good,' Imogen said. 'It's an excuse for me to leave him to it.'

'James is already out of it,' Nick said. 'It'll only get noisy and stupid.'

'Come with us,' Mark said. 'We're going back to my house. We're going to drink, chat and play canasta.'

'Oh, that sounds very nice and civilised. Stu and Kate would be up for that, I think. Then I can crash out at Stu's with Katie.'

'Or Jake could take you home,' Julie suggested.

Imogen looked over at Jake and Chrissie. 'I'm sure he has better things to do.'

Gray interrupted. 'Yes, tow me, for a start.'

'Do you and Chris want to come back to my place?' Mark said. Mark's older brothers had left home, and his parents were as tolerant as James's. As long as there was no loud music, and they only chatted and played games, they could all stay till dawn if they wanted.

Chris shook his head. 'When the car's back at Gray's I'd better make sure the battery and ignition leads are in the right place. Don't want to be burning the garage down.'

'No, we don't,' Gray said. 'I'm in enough shit.'

The bell behind the bar rang for last orders. Imogen was in no mood for more drink.

'I'm knackered,' Julie said. 'I need to go home.'

Mark had already finished his pint. 'Why don't we go now? We can walk you home.'

Simon nodded, and swigged down his orange juice. Nick tossed back the last of his vodka and coke. Imogen went over to Stuart and Kate. She squatted between them, glancing at Mark. They nodded, and then they finished their drinks and stood, saying goodbye to the others at the band table. Mark, Nick, Simon and Julie joined them while Imogen now squatted next to James, explaining to him what she was doing. James remonstrated; there was arm waving, and some petulance. Imogen shrugged, kissed James on the mouth and tousled his long hair. She then joined those going back to Mark's house. 'Right, I've done my best,' she said. 'Let's go.'

They left the bar, and walked down the steps and into the Market Place where Gray and Chris tied a rope between the Mini and Jake's Triumph. Simon wondered whether Jake should be driving. He wondered that most times Jake was in town. But then, Gray should probably not be steering.

Chris saw Simon. 'Hey, Si! See you tomorrow.'

Simon remembered then that he'd agreed to help Chris lift out the Vitesse's engine. 'Oh, yeah. See you sometime after dinner.'

The seven friends walked out of the Market Place, and onto Town Road. Julie lived at the very top of it, near where it entered into Barton Road. Mark lived further along Barton Road.

Julie and Simon had walked ahead of the others, who chatted behind them.

'It was a fun night,' Julie said. 'If... weird...'

'It was fun,' Simon said. '*And* very odd.'

'I'm glad you said I should come to the Lion. It was nice being with you all again.'

'*I'm* glad you listened to me.' Simon smiled. 'It was nice to see you in there again, Jules.'

A dark shape loped towards them. It was Greaser. 'Julie,' he said. 'Wow, man. Good to see you.'

Julie and Simon stopped. The others passed by slowly, and sauntered on along the road.

'Hello again, Greaser,' Julie replied.

Greaser looked at her and then at Simon. 'Have you got any dope? Speed? Anything?'

'You've already asked us this,' Julie said. 'Don't you remember seeing us earlier?'

Greaser looked around, confused. 'Have I?'

'Yes.'

'So... Do you?'

'No, Greaser. You should know we're the wrong people to ask for this.'

'Well, there's no harm in trying, is there. He looked around at the street, and the houses. 'I don't know why I'm here. I don't know anybody who lives at this end of town.'

'Not anybody with drugs, no, ' Julie said.

'Tim was looking for you.'

'You said that, too.'

'When?'

'When we met outside The Lion.'

Greaser nodded, slowly, then said, 'Did we?' He looked at Simon. 'What about you, mate?'

Simon shook his head. 'Sorry, Greaser, I don't do drugs. My

body is a temple, you know.' The others had slowly wandered a little further along the road. They didn't want to get caught up with Greaser. He'd only ask each of them if they had drugs.

'We have to get going, Greaser,' Julie said.

'Okay, yeah, right Jules. See you. If you do see Jeff, tell him Greaser's looking for him. And I'll tell Tim you were looking for him.'

Julie didn't bother to contradict him this time. 'See you later,' she said, and walked off purposefully. Simon followed.

'Who is this Jeff?' Simon said.

'A dealer. He drives down from Reading at least once a month.'

Simon and Julie caught up with the others, and Julie hurried them all along, to put some distance between herself and Greaser. They soon arrived at the gate to Julie's parent's house. Again, the others carried on slowly walking when Julie and Simon stopped. Julie took Simon's hand and led him through the gate to the front door. 'It's been great,' she said.

'Phone me if you want to go out again.'

Julie looked up at him, her face soft, tender. 'I might just do that.' She took a key out of her pocket and opened the front door. 'I'll see you soon.' She kissed his cheek then, and went through the door.

Simon felt a pleasant fluttering in his chest. He turned and jogged down the path to the pavement, and quickly caught up with his dawdling friends. Mark was talking to Stuart and Kate about Honeyhouse. Nick was talking with Imogen, but turned as Stuart caught them, and said: 'So, what happened to Anna, then?'

'What? What?' Simon said. 'What about Anna?'

'Exactly,' Nick said. 'What about Anna? You and Jules looked most comfy together.'

'Oh, don't be silly. She just needs somebody to talk to, that's all. There's nothing else to it. She's only just broken up with Tim, remember.'

Imogen nodded at Simon. 'Oh, we all know about Julie and Tim,' she said. 'And we all know about you and Anna. But Nick's right. You and Jules do look comfy.'

Simon was confused. He hadn't thought of Julie in that way, although her hand had felt good in his. And there had been the flutter in his chest. *What about Anna. Is she thinking of me?*

.

4

This is Below

THE FOOL.

Julie decided to call Simon. She had nothing going on that evening and would much rather see Simon than Tim.

'How about we meet up?' she said, when Simon had answered the phone.

'Yeah, that sounds good. So what shall we do?'

'Did you have a plan for tonight?'

'Well, I was going for a walk, with Mark and Nick. Up to Copsehill.'

'That actually sounds fun, you know. I haven't been on the hills for a long time.'

'And Imo and Kate will be there. '.

'So where are the boyfriends going?'

'Stuart and James have gone to Bath to see a horror movie. *The Omen*, I think it's called. Kate and Imo thought it sounded more than a little silly. James will, of course, want to hang out in the pubs afterwards.'

'Are we staying up the hill all night?'

'No, we're just going on a tour. We'll undoubtedly end up back at the White Lion later on.'

They agreed a time to meet up. Julie replaced the warm handset and fell to wondering what she should wear on this evening's excursion. She would need her sensible jeans – there might be nettles and thistles – and sensible shoes; she didn't want flints and stones between her toes. Then she renounced her sober self. It was Saturday – she should wear something nice, even on the hills. She could wear something Simon liked. But then she wondered why she would think that. Simon was always nice to her, no matter what she wore. She returned to the idea of jeans and a pair of baseball boots. She would wear her boat-neck striped top. She put it all on and checked herself in the wardrobe mirror. The top looked good. She twisted and turned. She knew Simon liked this top, he had once before remarked how nice she looked in it, back in the days when she had still been going out with Tim. Simon might like the top even more now as she wasn't with Tim.

She was hot, though. She took off the top and put on a light, white tee-shirt. She looked in the mirror again She didn't like it. And her arms would be exposed to the sun for hours as she walked across the hills. She took off the tee and pulled on the stripy boat-neck top again. She liked this top. And she liked that Simon would like it. Daringly, she removed her bra. She tried to remember when she had last gone out without a bra. She nearly always wore one now, except when she was lounging about the house, or when she rarely wore a halter top. But this was the 1970s, after all. Would it matter if she went without? She did feel better. Somewhat cooler. Less constricted. She wondered if anyone would notice how free she had become –

her breasts were small. She bounced on the balls of her feet. She definitely jiggled in a subtly different way. But the difference was, she decided, hardly noticeable. Only perverts would look that closely at her breasts, and they would look at her anyway. There was nothing she could do about leering men. They're silly, she thought. Dumb. She looked at the top in the mirror once more. It *was* nice.

She had an hour now to kill. She was meeting Simon and the others at the Lion. She went downstairs, and poured herself a cold orange juice from the fridge. Her parents were out, visiting her grandmother, and her sister was out with her latest boyfriend. She had the house all to herself. She went to the lounge and switched on the television. She pushed a button to change the channel. She found coverage of Wimbledon on BBC2 and settled down on the sofa to watch it.

During a tense first set tie-break, the telephone rang. Julie stood and went out to the dark hallway. She picked up the handset and was surprised to hear the voice of Tim. 'Do you want to go out tonight?'

Julie's heart tumbled, her stomach contracted. 'Why would I want to?'

'Because we were good together.'

'Don't you have any friends to hang around with down the pub tonight?'

'Of course I do. But I miss you. I want hang around with you.'

The phone call was unexpected. A conciliatory Tim was unexpected. What was also unexpected was what Julie said next. 'Not now.'

'We need to talk. I need to talk. I need to talk with you. Tonight.'

'I've already made arrangements. I don't want to let people down.'

'Who are you seeing tonight, then?'

'Just the old friends. Imo, Kate, Mark, Nick and Simon. The usual.'

'Somebody said they'd seen you out and about with Simon.'

'We were just hanging out together. We're both free in the afternoons. Don't you worry, nothing's happened.' Although, Julie thought, what she did with who was now none of Tim's business.

'I'm not worried,' Tim said.

Yes, you are. 'Look, I can't come out tonight, right? But we could meet up tomorrow, or later in the week. I'll phone.'

'Why not tonight?'

'Because I've already made plans to go out. And it'll be pleasant to spend an evening walking on the hills.'

'Walking?'

'Yes, walking. I know *you* don't walk much, but I've missed going for a nice walk over the hills.'

'Do you think I could come with you?'

'You don't want to go for a walk. And especially with people you think of as useless hippies.'

'Well, I'd do it for you, Julie.'

'No. I'm looking forward to this. I don't want any heavy vibes. I'll give you a call, Tim, all right?'

'All right. But make it soon, okay?'

'We'll see. 'Bye.' Julie replaced the handset. She was disturbed now, anxious. She paced around the house, picking things up and putting them down. There was adrenaline in her blood, an emptiness in her stomach, and her heart was beating faster than it should. Oh, damn Tim! Damn him! She had so wanted a pleasant evening with Simon and old friends. She had neither expected nor wanted Tim to cast a shadow over what she hoped would be a sunny, unclouded evening. She glanced at her wristwatch, a small oval on a slim leather strap. It was time to go. She looked in the wall mirror in the hallway. She ran her fingers through her blonde hair, attempting to give it body. The sticky heat of the afternoon had flattened it. She made a face at herself, and then she pouted. At least her mouth was nice. Interesting quizzical eyebrows. She knew she had nice blue eyes.

66

Many people had told her so, and not all of them relatives. She wasn't Imo or Heather, but then not many people were. She knew she wasn't *bad*-looking. After all, there had been Tim and Tony, and some other passing boyfriends. She pushed her hair up again, sighed as it fell back, and then left the house.

Swifts and swallows sketched the routes of rising thermals and sliced buttery yellow air beneath milky white clouds. Julie looked out across fields to the slopes of Derebury Hill. She had met the others in the pub, from where, after a drink or two, they had started their evening stroll. The streets of Dereham had been hot and muggy. They had walked along dusty White Street before striking off onto a footpath that led around the contours of Red Post Hill. As they followed the path higher up the hill, a breeze began to blow across the slopes. The breeze was warm, but welcome. The view, now they had reached the summit of Red Post Hill, was lovely, with downs, combes and copses spreading out to the horizon. The north side of the hill on which Julie stood sat higher than Copsehill, and its clump of trees squatted a mile or so to the north-east, thick with beech, field maple, and whitebeam. The hangings of Red Post Hill were limned with sheep walks, and chalk could be seen through the hoof-thinned grass. The well-worn path they followed cut a wide chalk-white and flint-grey line through long, drooping, brown and blonde grass that had been scorched by summer heat. Skylarks hollered into the sky and corn buntings jangled from posts.

Julie walked with Simon, slightly behind the others. For the moment, Nick had paired up with Kate, and they had walked on ahead. Mark and Imogen were talking, Julie knew – from fragments she had overheard – about Honeyhouse. Mark was suggesting again that Imogen should join the band. She refused, as always. Oddly, for one so confident, she was nervous on a stage. She had practiced with Honeyhouse a couple of times, and even that had been too much for her. She had once been in a local theatre group, but, she was so nervous she had been given very few lines.

'What are you reading?' Julie said. She knew that Simon liked to read. 'Anything good? Interesting?'

'*King Arthur's Avalon*,' Simon said. 'A little bit of history.'

'*King Arthur's Avalon?*'

'Yes. *King Arthur's Avalon*.'

Laughter began to bubble inside her. 'It sounds a bit like aftershave.' She made her voice deeper, husky. '*King Arthur's Avalon. For men*.'

Simon laughed. 'Do you stock it in Boots?'

'We should.' She lowered her voice again. '*Avalon*, by King Arthur. For the dark-age barbarian in *your* life.'

Simon made *his* voice deeper, and then said: 'After a day picking turnips or currying the old grey mare, you need *Avalon*. By King Arthur.'

'For *men*,' Julie added, and laughed. She threaded her arm through Simon's.

'Tim phoned earlier,' Julie said.

'Really? What did he want?' Simon asked.

'To see me.'

'When?'

'Tonight.'

'You're *here*.'

'Yes. I'd already made the plan to come on this walk with you guys. I've been looking forward to this walk.' *And seeing you*, she wanted to add. 'I didn't want to go chasing off after him like a chump.' She paused. 'It's too soon. I don't know what I want.' Perhaps it was Simon, she thought, glancing at his handsome profile as he walked beside her.

They walked along the ridge between the tops of Red Post and Copsehill. To the northwest the downs rolled slowly away from them, into the Vale of Pewsey. To the east, the hanging fell away sharply, and curved around a field below them – Tinker's Hole, dotted with sheep. A barbed wire fence ran along the top of the hanging, a few feet from its gentle, hummocky edge. A stonechat flew onto a post, flicking its tail, twisting its black head, its red breast bright in the setting sun. The bird quickly darted away, startled by the walkers nearby. Julie stopped by the fence where the hanging curved close to the path. She looked out over Tinker's Hole and the grey slate roof of Red Post Farm, across green fields where black and white Friesian cows tugged at the brown grass, to the slopes of Derebury Hill. She could see people lying on the distant embankments, smudges against the green, children running down into the ditches, moving spots against the chalk, and teenagers, silhouetted against a sky all hazy yellow, flying a kite near a round barrow. From where she stood she could hear the squeals and shouts from the other hill. A breeze crawled up the steep slope from Tinker's Hole, played at the edges of Julie's sailor top and slipped beneath it, cooling her pale skin, lifted the top and slid around her breasts, before gliding over her back and then away across the downs towards the setting sun. Warm and loose-limbed, she relaxed here on the lip of the high hanging. The evening light had turned to gold, and the blue of the sky shaded to red, orange, turquoise, azure.

Julie began to walk again, soon catching the dawdling Simon. The others had now walked far ahead. Kate and Mark had stopped for a fag. Imo was leaning against a tree, deep in conversation with Nick.

'Does Gray have a car yet?' Julie said. 'You were going to help Chris, weren't you? '

'I *were!*' Simon said. 'The engine's out. Skinned a few knuckles, but I survived. I saw Chris yesterday, and he's stripped the engine down already.'

'So, Gray can't drive anywhere, yet?'

'Only in his kiddie's Mini. And he's not risking that again. He was looking down in the mouth about it all the last time I saw him.'

'He needs a woman, not a car. Perhaps we should find one for him.'

'Well, perhaps *you* can find him one. I know of no unattached girls. Although...What about Sarah?'

'She's off men.'

'Oh well. I'll leave it up to you.'

They walked in silence for a few steps.

'So, then,' Simon said. 'Tim... And you. What are you going to do? Any ideas?'

Julie thought she could hear concern in Simon's voice. Concern about what, though? That she'd return to Tim? That, by doing so, he wouldn't have the chance to go out with her?

'I don't know, Si. It's all a bit confusing for me. It's different.'

'But you left him, right? So you can't have enjoyed being with him that much.'

'Oh, he made me happy enough. We had some fun.'

Simon frowned. 'So why did you split?'

'He could be a little selfish. He wanted to do his own things. I don't know. Perhaps because he didn't like to do all *this*. The walking, the talking, you know...'

Simon and his friends had their charms. They were bright. They were witty and most droll. Sometimes it seemed as though they spoke in code, and then Julie didn't quite understand the jokes. But they were relaxed, they were *cool*. All the people she knew through Tim were becoming *uncool*. Greaser and his need for cocaine, Dodgy Len handling stolen goods, Frank and Phil becoming gangsters. That world was a little darker than the one that Simon lived in. Tim's world had its own excitements. But Simon's world was sunnier, and full of possibility. His world was like this summer. She sensed that moving in Tim's world would soon become limiting, even if she was more likely to go parachute jumping, or to the races, or to a posh restaurant, or to a Grand Prix. Julie wasn't quite sure how much she wanted those things, anyway, especially if they meant being part of a shady, slightly dangerous world. Equally, she was not certain how much she wanted the laid back, slow world of Honeyhouse and friends. Yet she felt very relaxed out here on the hills with

70

Simon. These summer days were bright, unclouded and open, yet her mind was clouded, her thoughts confused, her wants unknown, her future obscure, uncertain.

She took Simon's hand. 'Look, Si, I don't know what's going on, especially with me and Tim. All I know is I'm happy here with you.' She looked down the path. 'And with them.' As she said that, warmth flowed through her, and she became even more relaxed. Worrying and thinking about serious things got her nowhere. And not out here, not this evening. She liked Simon. She liked his deep blue eyes and the crinkle around them when he smiled at her bad jokes. She liked the long fair hair he was always brushing away from his face. She liked the way he walked – tall, strong. She kissed him on the cheek. Simon turned to her. 'And what was that for?'

'For listening. For your patience. For being handsome. More handsome.'

'More handsome?' Simon said. 'Than what?'

'Than the other one. Than yesterday. Than most.'

Simon laughed. 'Oh yes, right, that's me. Handsome Simon they call me.'

'I'm sure they do... when you're not there.'

They caught up with the other friends. Julie kissed Simon's cheek again, and then threaded her arms through those of Kate and Imogen, before she led them away from the boys.

'Now, why don't we have some girl talk,' Julie said. She was happy to be back with her old friends, the ones she had known before Tim. 'So,' she said to Kate. 'What's this about you and Stuart?'

Kate smiled. 'We're together.'

'Is it good?'

'It *is* good,' Kate said. 'We're having fun together.'

Kate was the same height as Julie, with long, dark, straight hair and brown eyes. She wasn't as intimidating as Imogen could sometimes be when you compared yourself with her. Kate seemed to inhabit the same kind of ordinary world that Julie did. The boys liked Kate. And she had liked the boys right back. Kate was the most experienced of them all. She could be funny. Given the mess that was her family, this was surprising. Her father had died when she was only eight, and her mother had married and divorced twice since then, one marriage lasting as little as six months. The youngest of the family, Kate had been more affected by her father's death than her brother and sister. Her brother, five years her senior, had cried for a month and then joined the Army. Her sister, ten years older than her, was already married and living down in Kent. Both her brother and sister were irregular visitors to the house, and were unaware that their mum coped marvellously with young Kate, and with being a young bereaved single mother, by swallowing antidepressants and drinking copious amounts of gin and tonic. Still, Kate had survived – although, Julie suspected, Kate had a need to be needed, a desire to be seen and embraced, a wish to be part of a social group. Imogen had always been Kate's best friend – they had grown up in the same village, gone to the same schools – and when Imogen had started seeing James, Kate had felt alone.

'But Stuart, eh?' Julie elbowed Kate playfully. 'Quite a catch, what? Imo and I were talking only yesterday about the lovely trinity that is Stuart and Simon and James. Hairy bastards.'

'Well, yes,' Kate said. 'They're all rather lovely. And what about you, Jules? Are you making a play for Si? That would be rather excellent. We could all spend time together.'

Julie glanced over her shoulder. Simon was deep in conversation with Mark and Nick about something. He gesticulated as he made some point to them. 'I don't know what I'm doing yet. I don't think he knows what he's doing. So I'm just going with the flow. I do like being with you all.'

Kate unlinked her arm so that she could find her pack of cigarettes. She took them from a pocket in the blue waistcoat she was wearing and offered one to Julie. Kate's family, like Imogen's, had money. Kate could therefore buy a better class of cigarette than Julie would normally smoke. Julie took a Dunhill, which Kate lit for her with a Zippo. She thanked Kate, and enjoyed the first deep draws on it, the taste of it. The cigarette was king-size and would last longer than one of her stubby little Player's Number 6. She wanted to smoke it slowly. Imogen had drifted away, had resumed her walk with the boys. Julie used this moment to link her arm with Kate's and resume walking. She wanted to talk to Kate. She walked more quickly now, creating space between them and the others.

'Are you happy with Stu?' Julie said.

'Oh yes. I've liked him for ages. Since I met him at party at Imo's. You were there, as well.'

Julie remembered. She'd been there, eighteen months ago, with Tony. He was two years older than her. He had left Dereham to go to York University. Up north. Her relationship with Tony had quickly collapsed as he fell for the amorous advances of a sexually voracious and oh! so *mature* second-year. 'So you've been waiting a little while to get your hands on your man,' Julie said.

'Oh, you know me. I never wait. Stuart was in that on-off thing then, with Lolly, his first girlfriend. Do you remember her? Lolly?'

Julie thought back, Lolly. Lorraine. A mixed-up army kid who'd left town with that druggie freak she had also been seeing, Greaser's mate, what was his name? She'd forgotten. 'She was seeing somebody else as well, though, wasn't she? The minx.'

'Yeah, Col. They went down to live in Glastonbury, I think. For the vibes, man.' She flipped the hippie peace sign and pulled a face. 'Although, as she only spread bad vibes, it was just as well she took off. By the time she did, however, I was with Barry. Kind of happy. Thinking it would last forever.'

'It didn't last long though, did it?'

'No, we split up. He was boring.'

'He said you were great, as I recall.'

73

Kate laughed. 'He lost his virginity with me, so has fond memories. His fond memories don't make him in any way more interesting. He'll find somebody suitable and be married off in a trice.'

'So then there was... Will, wasn't it?'

'Yes. If Simon hadn't buggered off down to Devon to visit Paul that week, I might have had a chance to get reacquainted with him.'

'Oh, poor Katie. Alas! Poor Stu.'

'So. Will turned out to be a shit.'

'And then you were free to chase Stu.'

'Well, Will was, what, a year ago? And you know Imo and Stu have always been so very close.'

Julie nodded. This was what she had been nudging Kate towards.

'So I thought that Imo and Stu were going to get together. And I like them both, and I thought that would be cool. Stu and Imo! I could hold no grudge against them. So that's when I went out with Miles.'

'They didn't get together though.'

'No, they dated a few times, but...'

'Did they... you know...'

'I think I do.' Kate winked. 'No, I don't think they did. She was a virgin until James. That's what she's always told me.'

'And afterwards?'

Kate looked puzzled. 'After what? What do you mean?'

'After those two got together. They've split up a couple of times since they went out. And as you say, Stu and Imo were always close.'

'Oh, I see.' Kate paused. 'I don't *think* anything like that happened.'

'Charlie thinks there's monkey business.'

Kate looked grave. 'How do you know that?'

'Imo said something. When I met her the other day in the pub.'

'Well.' Kate paused. 'Charlie *is* crazy. He always thought James was just a passing fancy for Imo, and that Stu would win her in the end. He hates that idea.'

'But Charlie's with Jane now, isn't he? Devon Paul's little sister.'

'Yes, young, distant Jane. Imo thinks that'll help Charlie get over her. Fat chance, is what I say to that.'

They arrived at the large stand of trees atop the summit of Copsehill. Kate offered Julie another cigarette which Julie gratefully accepted. Julie would offer Kate one of her cigarettes in return later. It was unlikely to be accepted, however, for which she was grateful. If you have a pack of Dunhill in your pocket, why would you smoke a Number 6?

The others soon caught up with them, frustrating Julie's efforts to discover any more secrets about Stuart and Imogen. They walked in and out of the copse, talking about the upcoming party at Mark's house, gossiping about girlfriends and boyfriends, and their other friends.

'This is where I first flirted with Stuart,' Kate said.

'Oh?' Julie said.

'Yes, back in April. I came on a skywatch. My first ever.'

'Did you see anything?' Simon said.

'Nothing,' Kate said. 'Oh, yes! Some flares!'

Imogen chuckled indulgently. 'James's brandy caught on fire.'

'And Charlie's sleeping bag.' Kate said. She too smiled at the memory.

'It sounds like a classic,' Mark said.

'Oh, it was. James was very drunk,' Imogen said. 'And he was stoned.'

'And so was Charlie,' Kate added.

'Stu and Charlie almost came to blows,' Imogen said. 'Fisticuffs.'

Kate's eyes widened. 'They did? But why?'

'Oh! That was meant to be secret. Ignore me. I said nothing.' Imogen blushed a little now.

Julie supposed that if Charlie wanted to fight Stuart it was something to do with Charlie's obsession with Imo and Stuart. None of the others felt the need to ask Imogen anything about the fight. They all knew the situation with Charlie. They began walking down the track towards the road back into town.

Julie took Simon's arm again. 'Are you going to Mark's party?'

'I can't imagine I'll be doing anything else,' he said. 'Almost everyone we know will be there.'

'As long as Tim isn't,' Julie said.

'Well, it's possible he'll come, of course. Tim is a friend of the many friends that Mark will surely invite.'

'Yes, good point. Well, I'll ignore him if he does arrive.'

'I shouldn't worry about it. He's very unlikely to come.'

'You're right. He'd probably prefer to go to a disco. He thinks you're all silly hippies, anyway.'

'Us? Silly hippies?'

'Kung fu? Tai chi? UFOs? The occult? Drugs *and* drink? You also read books, all of you. You're like... a bunch of decadent aesthetes, or... something like that, anyway.'

'Really? Hmm. *The Decadent Aesthetes.* I rather like the sound of that.'

'By the way, where's Gaz? 'Julie asked. 'I haven't seen him for ages. He usually hangs around with you guys, doesn't he?'

'He's being most mysterious.' Simon said. 'We haven't seen him quite as much as we're used to. He claims that work has worn him out.'

'Oh, poor boy.'

'Well, weird boy, more like. Still,' Simon said, 'I'm sure he'll be at the party next week. I can't imagine he'd miss that.'

'Who would want to miss that,' Mark said.

The Honeyhouse gang would be there, Julie thought, and so would The Prophets and their friends. Then there would be those connected directly with Mark and his friends, like Chrissie and Jake, and herself and Sarah, and the friends they too would inevitably bring along. Tim *would* find out. She could only hope he wouldn't come.

Nick was looking down the rough track. 'There are people at the white gates.'

Julie also looked down the track. The twilight was deepening now. She could see torch light and dark shapes moving about the road below.

'Skywatchers, I reckon' Mark said.

Simon climbed over the white gate, and then helped Julie climb over. She stood in front of him, smiling. She wasn't quite sure why. She liked Simon. She liked these friends. The evening was warm and lovely. The sky was a deep, cobalt blue.

Simon was looking at her top. 'That's a... uh... nice top. I've always liked that top. That... top... always looks good on you.'

'Thank you,' Julie said. It wasn't like Simon to be all tongue-tied. *He's noticed I'm not wearing a bra.* Her smile widened.

'You're grinning like a loon,' Simon said.

'I'm enjoying myself. It's nice to be with you.' Julie turned to the skywatchers as their friends climbed over the gate.

The skywatchers greeted them. Have you seen anything?' one asked. The question was customary, part of an almost ritual exchange between all skywatchers. The *anything* enquired after was, of course, a shining UFO, the chimera that brought the faithful to the hill weekend after weekend, year after year, chasing a dream.

'Nothing,' Simon said. 'Not a thing.' He looked up at the sky. 'A nice night for a skywatch, though.'

The skywatcher also looked up. 'Yes, it's lovely. What a summer.'

'It's been fantastic,' Julie said. 'The last few days have been the best.'

'They certainly have,' Simon said. 'Are you staying here all night?' he asked the skywatchers.

'Oh, yes,' a skywatcher with long hair said. 'We've come up from Surrey.' His friends were removing sleeping bags, and bags full of drinks and food from an old yellow Hillman Imp. 'We're a part of a small UFO group, Surrey Direct Investigations. Do you all live around here?'

'Yes,' Simon said. 'We like to walk around these old hills at night.'

Julie took out her cigarettes, and offered one of them to Kate, who shook her head, preferring, just as Julie had expected, the silky smoothness of her Dunhill. Mark, however, said he'd like one. She'd have to get one in return from him later. Mark struck a match and lit all the cigarettes.

Julie took a deep drag, and then said, 'I've never seen a UFO.'

'No, neither have I,' Simon said.

The long-haired skywatcher was shocked. 'Never?'

Simon shook his head. 'I don't think any of us have. Have you, Nick?'

Nick said he hadn't, and Kate said she'd only been on one skywatch. Mark filled the sky with his blue smoke. 'I thought I saw something once but it turned out to be a glider shining in the afternoon sun. And what about you, Imogen? You and James come here more often than any of the rest of us.'

'Oh, we've seen some lights in the sky, but I'm loath to think of them as anything extraordinary.'

She was *loath to think of them as anything extraordinary*. Julie replayed Imogen's last utterance a couple of times. She spoke so well. *I probably sound a right idiot compared to her.*

'We've seen all sorts.' A difference voice – another skywatcher with an Electric Light Orchestra tee-shirt.

'What? Here?' Nick wondered out loud.

'Not only here,' ELO-fan said. 'Although this place does have great vibes.'

'Great vibes, yeah, great,' the long-haired man said.

Julie wondered if the skywatchers would roll up a fat one after she and the rest left them alone, would chill out and feel the vibes, man. She had always wondered about the vibes. She had been walking over Copsehill since she was young, and had felt nothing except the joy at the simple exuberant beauty of it all on a clear spring day with hawthorn and blackthorn in flower and an unclouded view over Derebury. She knew that wasn't what the skywatchers meant. But she'd felt more vibes in the dark woods near Black Dog, where a lantern-eyed Labrador was rumoured to roam, than she'd ever experienced here.

'So, no weird incidents at *all*?' The long-haired skywatcher said.

Simon and his friends shook their heads. 'We're not *believers*,' Simon said.

'Ah, well, if you'd seen the things We'd seen, you'd believe,' ELO-fan said.

No-one asked what the Surrey group had seen. If somebody did, they might be trapped here for hours, regaled with tales of lights in the sky, strange sounds on the chalk track and invisible walkers in the copse.

'They respond to psychic vibes, man,' the long-haired skywatcher proclaimed.

'Yeah, right on,' said a skywatcher who hadn't yet said anything.

'You might emit negative vibes,' the long-haired man said.

'We always attempt to create the right mind-set for skywatching,' the fan of ELO said.

'We could teach you how to get there,' the long-haired man said.

'Uh, thanks,' Simon said. 'But no time. We're on our way to the pub.'

'What? The *pub*?' ELO-man said, scornfully. 'When you could be out *here*? In all *this*?'

Mark dropped his cigarette-end to the ground. 'Well, we're up here a lot,' he said. 'And on Derebury Hill. And on the Plain.' He waved, then turned and walked away.

'Have a good evening,' Julie said.

'I'm sure there'll be others along to share your vigil,' Simon said. 'Keep vibrating. You never know what you might see.'

The others had walked on ahead. Simon and Julie turned to follow.

'You don't believe in UFOs, then,' Julie said.

'No, never have done,' Simon said. 'I can't believe they'd fly all this way and then interact so very little. Oh, and the photos have always been so very, very bad. You?'

'Well, I kind of want to believe. It would be cool if aliens were coming here to observe us.'

'A kind of replacement for God.'

Julie considered the idea. 'No, no. They couldn't replace God.'

'Do you believe there's a God?'

'Oh, I don't know. It's confusing. Why would God make a world like this? Bad people, pain, and suffering.' She shook her head. 'I once believed...'

'So you've become an atheist?'

'Not really. What's that other word?'

'Agnostic? Sitting on the fence.'

Julie looked at Simon, nodded. 'You're an atheist, right?' she said.

'I certainly am,' Simon said.

Julie sighed. 'I don't know what I believe.' She hoped there was something that would make sense of everything – why we were here, how we should live, how we should treat other people. But perhaps that *something* was *people*. And if it was about people, then perhaps it should also be all about love. She could believe in love. That seemed real. Very real. It might be a little corny, she supposed, to so simply believe in love – all very hippie and temple-bells. She hoped one day that she could love someone deeply and completely, and that he would return her love. There would be marriage, and children. There would be happiness and play, conversation, and intimacy. There would be sharing and memories made together. Could Tim give her all of that? She didn't think so. Could Simon? She didn't know that, yet, either.

Still, she took Simon's hand as they walked down the hill towards town.

5
This is Behind

Simon had been at Mark's most of the day, with Nick and Gaz, helping set up the party. This had involved moving to the garage ornaments that must never be broken, rearranging some furniture, drinking, moving more ornaments and more drinking, playing loud music, having a sing-song while Mark played the guitar, cups of coffee, biscuits, and wondering who would come tonight.

Heather was heading over from Southleigh. She and Nick were now going out together. Simon liked Heather. Gaz had been happy to hear that Heather's friend Mary was coming. Gaz had taken a fancy to Mary. Simon had observed Gaz and Mary a couple of times when they had met up, and believed she had no interest in him. Gaz was, Simon suspected, way too smooth. But then, Mary cultivated an hauteur, a kind of distant, airy affectedness. There was nothing that Mary didn't like, and yet she also disliked everything she considered old-fashioned, and infra dig. She would undoubtedly find the music, the tastes, the conversation, and the people at the party not to her taste at all.

There was no chance Anna would arrive at Mark's this evening, which was disappointing. However, Simon knew Julie would come, and looked forward to seeing her. He liked the simple intimacy that had grown between them, even if he wasn't sure where that familiarity might lead. He enjoyed his conversations with her. He liked that he could take and hold her hand. He liked that he could blithely put an arm across her shoulders or around her waist. Julie would reciprocate with a smile and bright eyes. Beyond these gestures nothing else had happened. They touched, but maintained a certain distance. Their intimacies only went so far, each held back, no doubt, by confusion about their previous relationships.

The sun shone brightly. Mark had drawn curtains over the windows, which were wide open in a futile attempt to cool the house. The room remained sticky and sultry.

'It's going to be a hot night, tonight,' Simon said.

'I hope so,' Gaz said. 'Then the girls won't wear much.'

'Perve,' Nick said.

'They could be naked, and still your chances with them would be nil,' Mark said.

'Yes, but if they were naked,' Gaz said, 'at least I'd finally see a naked lady.'

'Which would indeed be a first,' Nick noted.

'Outside of a magazine,' Mark added.

Gaz shrugged, and then pouted. 'Better than nothing.'

Nick looked through Mark's record collection. Hawkwind. Wishbone Ash. Led Zeppelin. Yes. 'Haven't you got *anything* we can dance to?'

'Dance?' Mark said. 'What do you think this is, a ruddy discotheque full of beat tunes for young people?'

'I know,' Nick said, 'that you've never been much of a dancer-' Gaz's snort of derision interrupted him. 'But the naked girls will never dance to these hippie epics.'

'Don't worry,' Mark said. 'Tradition dictates that the fairer sex brings their own music. Everyone knows what my musical tastes are. Chrissie always brings dancing music with her.'

'Julie will, too' Simon said. 'She phoned me yesterday and asked if Mark had any music other than, she said, and I quote-'

Nick interrupted Simon. 'Verbatim?'

'*Ish*,' Simon said. 'I quote, verbatim-*ish*-'

'Excellent,' Nick said.

'Head-banging nonsense,' Simon continued, 'that meanders on meaninglessly for more minutes than necessary in any universe.'

'Most poetic,' Gaz said. 'Will Jules be naked?'

'I don't think so ' Simon said. He recalled fondly, though, the sailor top she'd worn last week, and how little she had on beneath it.

Simon had seen Julie a couple of times during the week, but only briefly. She was looking forward to the party, she said. He had spent the last few days wondering what Anna was up to, and whether she still thought of him. But then he would smile to himself, distracted by thoughts of Julie, and her stripy top, remembering something she'd said, or the feel of her hand in his. And then he would become confused and wonder what he should do, or should be doing.

Simon had made discreet enquiries, but nobody could be sure whether Tim would turn up at the party this evening. Many uninvited people would end up at the party anyway, especially after the pubs had closed. They always did. Invites were unnecessary; the only requirement was that attendees should bring a bottle – and a full one. And most did. Some managed to sneak past the gatekeepers, who were usually Nick,

Mark and Simon or other trusted friends. Nick and Simon rarely got drunk, and Mark usually tried to stay sober for his parties so he could keep an eye on the party-goers and ensure little damage to the house occurred. Simon hoped Tim wouldn't sneak in and demand to see Julie. Simon rather wanted her to himself.

As expected, Chris and Gray, The Prophets, and the Honeyhouse gang had arrived first. James brought with him two bottles of Martell. James's intention had been, no doubt, to heroically drink them both himself, but Imogen had grabbed one of the bottles as soon as they'd arrived and poured large measures into cups and glasses for her, Stuart and Kate. Charlie was the only Prophet missing. Kate said he was in Devon, visiting the lovely Jane. Danny was already stoned. He had already smoked a joint or two to get himself *in the mood*. John had brought along two bottles of Strongbow. Simon wasn't much of a drinker but he had liberated a bottle of Martini Rosso from his parents, who had bought it at Christmas but never opened it. Simon liked Martini and lemonade.

Jake and Chrissie were the next to arrive. Mark was often distant with Jake, who was, after all, going out with Chrissie, and Chrissie was Mark's one true, hopeless love - but Jake acted as though he never noticed, and brought with him two cans of Party Seven. Chrissie had brought with her a selection of singles, as she'd promised and now Nick looked through them, sometimes nodding approvingly.

The party was in its early stages. Simon rather liked the atmosphere of these quiet moments. Pink Floyd drifted quietly from the speakers. Everybody was affable and sociable. The drink had lubricated friendships rather than removed inhibitions. The latter state would occur for most somewhere between eleven and one o'clock tonight. And then, after one o'clock, would come aggression, nausea or remorse - and, perhaps, all three.

The doorbell rang. At the moment the door remained closed to arbitrary entry, but later access would be easier, and the gatekeepers would need to be alert. Mark returned with Heather and Mary. Nick greeted Heather with a kiss. Gaz looked at Mary hopefully, but she headed straight for the singles and albums. Nick introduced Heather and Mary. Except for a brief nod at the first name, Mary concentrated on the records. Simon wondered if Mary ever let her mask of cool indifference slip. She studied the records, but he couldn't imagine she would find many to interest her. She didn't appear to be the kind of girl who would admire Mark's prog-rock collection, nor the disco, pop and soft rock that Chrissie and Julie would bring to the party. He couldn't imagine her dancing to *Heaven Must be Missing an Angel*. David Bowie, The Velvet Underground, Lou Reed and Iggy Pop would be her bag.

The doorbell rang again. Mark answered it. He returned with Julie ahead of him. Julie handed Mark a bagful of singles. Simon stood and embraced her, then kissed her cheek. She melted into him for a moment. He didn't know when this had become a thing, their thing, this hugging, kissing and melting, but somewhere, somehow, in the last few weeks of meeting up in the lazy, sultry, sunshine, something had happened between them. They parted, and she winked at him and grinned. She then said hello to everybody, hugged Imogen and Kate and some others, but it was, of course, a different kind of hug to the one still impressed into Simon's body. Nick introduced her to Heather and Mary. She and Heather exchanged a few pleasantries about meeting each other in The Swan.

'Right, I need a drink,' Julie finally said.

Simon followed Julie into the kitchen. She wore a long, flouncy, lacy, gypsy skirt, and a loose, yellow, scoop-necked tee-shirt with sleeves that flared at the wrist. She had a smiley pendant on a thong around her neck. She looked gorgeous. Julie said hello to Danny and John, who had migrated to the kitchen without anybody else noticing. Simon wondered if one of them was dealing. Julie looked at various bottles before deciding on a glass of Simon's Martini. Simon poured the drink and handed it to her, then took his hand and led him back into the sitting room, where they rejoined the others.

When *Dark Side of the Moon* had finished, Chrissie had reached the record deck before any of the boys, and James Taylor's voice now wafted out of the speakers. Julie lit a cigarette, and sipped her Martini. Mark pulled back the curtains. The sun was setting, and the parched garden glowed golden through the open French windows at the back of the room.

Still nobody danced. Well, it was rather early in the evening yet, Simon thought. The head-banging and dancing were still to come. His friends chatted, drank and smoked, draped themselves languidly over sofas and each other, languorous and limp in the still, hot evening. Julie leaned back against Simon's shoulder. Imogen leaned against James. Kate sat in Stuart's lap. Nick and Heather were kissing. Gaz was attempting to talk to Mary. Mark stood occasionally to let people in.

'Do you think Tim will arrive?' Simon said.

Julie shrugged. 'I hope not. He would only get all heavy. And I don't want that.'

'Let's also hope, then, that he doesn't get tanked up down the Swan, and then come here.'

They both knew Tim liked a drink. He could be sociable and amusing when drunk, but if he drank too much he could turn nasty. Simon had once witnessed Tim falling out, and then falling about, with somebody outside The Swan. There had been some pushing and shoving, and a couple of misdirected haymakers that fell on shoulders and arms rather than on the face at which the blows had been aimed. Simon had seen nothing he couldn't handle, although he wouldn't want such a scene at Mark's party, where it would ruin the night.

Tim wouldn't come. Simon really hoped that Tim wouldn't come. *Surely*, he wouldn't come. Julie was sitting up now, and talked to Imo. They chatted about Charlie, who was down in

Devon with Paul and, of course, with Jane. Imogen said that Charlie was obsessive. Julie said she sometimes found Charlie odd. Simon watched Julie as she talked. He liked her voice. It was soft, with a lilt. A west Wiltshire lilt. He liked her nose, too. Small, upturned. He liked her fine, blonde hair. He felt the need to move some of her hair away from her face and behind a small ear. He did so. There was a flutter behind his ribs. Julie kissed his cheek. Something fluttered again. Julie continued talking to Imo. Simon looked around him. Kate was on Stuart's knee. She gave Simon a meaningful look. Simon couldn't quite fathom what the meaning was. Everyone was talking to everyone. Outside the French window the evening had long faded to a still twilight. The sky was a deep blue, shading to black, and stars were now beginning to appear.

More people had arrived while Simon had been sitting with Julie, happily watching the party unfold. James Taylor had been replaced with the music Chrissie and Julie had brought with them. The music had slowly become much louder. The room was lit by candles and nightlights which Mark had lit as the dark of evening had deepened. The room was hazed with smoke from cigarettes and joss-sticks, and the room was scented with patchouli, ambergris and sandalwood.

Year of the Cat was now playing. Julie looked at Simon. 'Shall we dance?'

'I don't know whether I can,' Simon said.

'Just think of it as tai chi. Fast tai chi.'

Julie pulled Simon up. *She doesn't give you time for questions*, Al Stewart sang. He followed Julie into the centre of the room, and started dancing. He knew he could dance, really. He had rhythm. But he still felt slightly foolish, as he always did at first, especially as the only other people dancing were Imo and Chrissie, who both danced well. It was a long song; as the four of them danced, others joined them. Simon became less self-aware, and enjoyed both the movement, and that Julie was dancing with him. She was happy and lost in the music. *You*

Make Me Feel Like Dancing now played, and at this moment that was how Julie made Simon feel. Simon would rarely listen to a single like this; only at a party could he be encouraged to dance around a beige carpet to such a song. Julie was joining in with the chorus as she danced, singing exuberantly, in a high voice, just like Leo Sayer. When *S S S Single Bed* started, Simon could imagine himself nowhere but on this carpet, on this night, with Jules. At this moment, there was only this moment, this movement, and blonde, *so*-happy Julie in her yellow sunshine tee-shirt and peasant skirt singing and shimmying and spinning.

Julie took his hands and they danced closer. Sometimes, she pulled herself in towards him. Sometimes, she twirled herself beneath his arm. She and Simon entertained each other by pretending they really could dance, emulating most ineptly moves they'd seen on television and in films. They laughed. Another song finished and Julie fell laughing into Simon's arms. He kissed the top of her head. Chrissie had put on another single, fighting off Gaz who wanted Wishbone Ash, and Mary, who had at last found something, *Walk on the Wild Side*, in Julie's singles. 'Later,' Chrissie was saying. 'No, later,' she emphasized, as she guarded the deck.

I'm Not in Love filled the room. Julie danced again, slowly, still wrapped in Simon's arms, her body against his. Simon moved too, slipping into her rhythm, hips swaying with hers. And as they danced together time stood still and a choir of voices hovered over them in the candlelight and heat.

Julie smelled good. 'Nice perfume,' Simon said.

'Thanks,' Julie said softly in his ear. 'It's *King Arthur's Avalon*. For men.'

'Well, I'm glad one of us is a boy.'

'Are you calling me a boy?' Julie said.

Simon shrugged, still dancing. 'If the cap fits.'

Julie leaned back to look into his eyes. Her smile was cheeky. Her eyes were twinkling, a warm sapphire blue in the candlelight. 'You're funny,' she said. Then she leaned forward and kissed him quickly, but warmly, fully, on the lips. 'I kind of like you,' she said.

Simon had to kiss her back. And his kiss was also warm, and full, and lingered on her lips longer than her kiss had on his. 'And I kind of like you, too,' Simon said.

Julie favoured Simon with another smile. 'Careful now. Don't get too carried away.'

'Ha! Could we get any more passionate?'

Julie raised an eyebrow. 'Perhaps we should try.'

'Perhaps we should kiss again, and find out.'

They kissed again. Each kiss became longer. Tongues touched. Simon had kissed girls before, but not that often; he was, after all, shy with girls. Somehow, what he was doing with Julie felt *right*. He imagined this was how kissing should be. It had been so easy. No fuss, no bother. He had been dancing with her one moment, and then kissing her the next. Something had changed for him. New possibilities abounded. He kissed Julie's neck. She was one of them.

Simon and Julie had been kissing, and chatting, and drinking, for nearly three hours. Simon glanced at his watch. Twenty to twelve. The pubs were closed now. The next half an hour was the period of maximum risk. Simon had already been called upon to help Mark refuse entry to Greaser. Not that Greaser had been too much trouble. He had been mainly confused – as ever – about where he actually was, and should be. Simon told him that he'd actually been invited over to Dodgy Len's, and reminded him of the address. Greaser was happy with Simon's invention, and wandered into the night, talking aloud. There'd been no trouble since then – all arrivals had been expected, and all had brought bottles.

For the last half an hour or so, someone other than Chrissie and Mark had been in control of the record player, and the music had become heavier and much louder. Simon and Julie went to the garden, leaving Gaz and some others to head-bang. Simon heard Wishbone Ash and then Hawkwind. He and Julie sat on the paving stones of the patio next to the French window. Simon leaned his back against the warm bricks of the house. Julie sat between his legs. His arms encircled her waist. His head was on her shoulder. It was a rather perfect position, Simon found, for kissing Julie's neck. He'd taken rather a fancy to her neck. James and Imo, and Nick and Heather also sat outside in the warm garden. Julie smoked one of James's black Sobranie. The evening remained cloudless and sultry. The mood of the party, particularly in the garden, was relaxed, unhurried. James and Nick talked about the occult. Imogen and Heather had never met, and were now getting to know each other. Gaz was still attempting to flirt with Mary, who appeared to tolerate Gaz's arm around her waist only for Heather's sake. Mary and Heather came as a pair, Simon thought. It was an unwritten rule he'd noted among the mysterious sisterhood of single girls. If Heather was to go out with a Dereham boy, then Mary should too – and, preferably, a close friend of Nick's. Despite Gaz's charms – which, Simon admitted were amusing, but few – Mary sat unkissed. As Gaz got closer, Mary backed away. Suddenly, she stood and said she would get drinks for everybody who wanted one. Gaz said he would go with her, but she said he should stay where he was and wait for her to come back. She walked briskly to the kitchen. She wasn't drunk, Simon saw, unlike Gaz.

'I think she likes me,' Gaz said wryly, and to no-one in particular.

Nick and Heather had started kissing again, leaving Julie to explain things to Gaz.

'You see your friend Simon here? You see me? Note how relaxed and lovely we both are. That is *liking* somebody. Sorry to say, Gaz, but Mary is supporting Heather.'

Heather and Nick stopped kissing. Heather looked at Gaz sympathetically. 'It's true,' she said. 'Mary wondered if there'd be any fanciable blokes here this evening. I told her about you, and that you were Nick's mate. She thought you might be worth a shot. But I have to tell you, you're out of luck.'

'Shame,' Gaz said. 'She's such a surly old cow. She absolutely is my kind of woman.'

Nick laughed. 'Well, that's what I said to Heather.'

Heather nodded. 'He said you two would be well suited. Trouble is, Mary's become far too cool over the last year. I'm afraid a head-banging weekend hippie like you isn't going to cut the mustard.'

'Oh well. Perhaps she'll be up for a one-night stand.'

'Ambition in adversity,' Simon said.

'You can't knock it,' Nick said.

'Well, I'll try,' Gaz said.

Chrissie still influenced the singles played, and now she put on Bread's *Make it With You*. Julie stood and pulled Simon up. 'Come on, kung fu boy, let's smooch 'til your boots fall off.'

Julie skipped as she led Simon to the lounge. The sentiments of David Gates agreed with those now experienced by Simon, who thought he might well be climbing on rainbows. As Julie relaxed into Simon's arms she brushed her smooth, warm cheek against his before gently bussing his lips with hers. Perhaps he should really make it with Jules. He hadn't thought about Anna all night. Well, not until this moment, at least, of thinking that he hadn't thought about her – but the important point was he *hadn't* thought about her in *that* way, which was *this* way. These moments with Julie, this kissing, the embracing, the holding and stroking were very real, and were things that had been very much missing from his short relationship with Anna. He leaned back and looked into Julie's eyes, which were, he thought – he hoped – bright with pleasure. She smiled up at him, and they kissed again. He'd almost asked her how she felt, but her eyes said it all. And kissing was much better than talking. After a few moments, they stopped kissing. Julie leaned her head against his shoulder as they continued circling the smoke-filled lounge, dancing now to *Sister Golden Hair*. He rested his cheek against Julie's head.

On their first turn about the room, Simon saw Mary talking to one of Jake's old friends. She leaned against the doorframe to the kitchen and toked on a joint. She was laughing. On their second circuit about the room, he spotted Chrissie and Jake, whose faces told him that they were about to descend into one of their squalling arguments. These usually involved Chrissie storming off, so Simon wasn't worried that they would fight. On their third circuit, Julie kissed him. On their fourth lazy peregrination, they stopped kissing, and Simon twirled Julie. Then Simon looked across Julie's blonde hair.

Tim stood at the door to the lounge, watching them.

6
This is Before

'Shit,' Simon said.

'Hmm?' Julie said, softly. 'What's up?'

'Tim,' Simon said. He danced Julie around until she faced towards the door.

'Shit,' Julie said into Simon's shoulder. 'I was enjoying myself, too.'

'So was I,' Simon said. He wasn't sure what Tim's arrival would mean, but it was certain to change everything about the evening.

Then Sarah entered from the hall. She said something to Tim. He put his arm around her, and guided her through the room. Simon wondered who had been the gate guard, though both Tim and Sarah carried bottles, so it didn't matter who was sentry – Mark, Nick, or another trusted friend – the bottles would guarantee their entry.

Julie caught sight of Sarah. 'What a cow!'

Tim nodded a greeting toward Julie, but Sarah looked down at the floor, blushing.

The last song had finished, and somebody other than Chrissie had taken control of the record player – Gaz, probably. Chrissie was too annoyed with Jake to notice. *The Boys are Back in Town* now blustered out. Simon and Julie no longer danced. Instead, Julie took Simon's hand, and led him quickly to the back garden. James and Imogen were still sitting there. James's head rested in Imogen's lap. 'Simon! Jules!' Imogen said. 'How excellent to see you both. Come sit with us.' Julie cursorily greeted her, but continued to lead Simon further into the garden. She managed to find a dark corner not occupied by others.

'What's going on in there, then?' Julie said.

'I don't know.' Simon said. But he could guess.

'Tim! Sarah!'

'I know. But does it matter?'

'Sarah! She's meant be my friend! So yes! Of course it matters to me! The cow...'

Tim's arrival had changed everything. The radiance had gone from the party now. The night was now simply heavy, humid. And Simon missed the hugging already. It had been only a few minutes since the last embrace, perhaps ten since the last kiss. Simon suspected that if those were not the last hugs and kisses of the evening, any he received from now on would have a different feeling, a different purpose, and would be given for a different reason.

'He wants to make you jealous,' Simon said.

'Well, of course,' Julie replied. 'But Sarah! What is she doing? What is she thinking?'

94

'Come on, Jules,' Simon said. 'You're not with Tim. You didn't want him here. You've been kissing me. You seem to like it. So, why do you care? What does it matter?'

'I don't understand why Sarah would do this. I didn't even know she fancied Tim.'

'Just let it go. Enjoy the rest of the night.' With me, Simon thought. Enjoy it with me. He wanted to kiss Julie some more.

'I need to talk to Sarah,' Julie said.

Simon could see Sarah through the windows. Her arms were around Tim's neck as they danced to the latest record Chrissie had put on the record player. Ironically, it was *I'm Not in Love*.

'I've been wearing this song like a stole lately,' Julie said quietly.

The song finished, and Tim kissed Sarah. It was a short kiss. Julie kissed Simon's cheek, then. 'Don't go away,' she said. 'I *will* be coming back for you.'

Julie squeezed Simon's hand, and then walked to the door. Simon sat down beside James and Imogen. James's head was still in Imogen's lap, but his eyes were closed. Imogen looked down at him, and then back up at Simon. 'He's just having a little rest for now.'

Simon frowned. 'I take it James is pissed? I thought I saw you guys trying to help him out with the brandy.'

'We did,' Imogen said. 'I'm tipsy, though. Kate and Stu have gone for a walk to sober up. The trouble is, there's plenty of drink here.' She stroked James's long hair back from his face. 'He's tried most of it this evening.' Imogen looked towards the French windows. 'I see trouble brewing.'

'Yes,' Simon said. 'I don't quite know what's going on there.'

'It's a shame Tim and Sarah arrived. You and Julie were looking good in there.'

'You've been watching?'

'For yonks. When Stu and Kate went for their walk, and James finally crashed out on me, my only entertainment was watching you and Jules. You'd make a lovely couple.'

Simon was surprised. 'We would? You think so?'

'Oh, yes. Very much. I was trying to think of a word to describe you both.'

'And what pithy word did you come up with?'

'*Genial*. Very genial. Being with you both would be warm, and friendly. I've missed Julie since she began hanging around with that iffy crowd in The Swan.'

'Genial.' Simon felt a smile building. It was even a most genial word. 'We'd make you tea when you came to visit.'

'You'd have cakes too. And a cat. And a vase on the table, with gay flowers in it... It would be a round Habitat table with a blue-checked tablecloth across it. You'd sit close together on the sofa and chat and laugh and make your friends feel very welcome.'

'You do make it sound very pleasant.'

'Your house would be the centre for us all. People would say *Let's go see Si and Jules*. Every visit with you would be *genial*.' Imogen did make that world sound fine.

Simon looked across to the French windows, and could see Julie talking to Sarah. Gaz regained control of the record player, and *Brainstorm* chugged out of the speakers.

'Tonight is the first time this summer that I've managed not to think about Anna,' Simon said. 'Jules and Tim were together for a year. It's going to be much harder for her.'

Imogen nodded. 'What about Anna?'

Simon looked through the French windows again. Julie followed Sarah across the room frowning, talking, gesticulating. 'I don't know. Who knows what she's been doing this summer? Perhaps she's at a party tonight, kissing somebody. Perhaps she's forgotten about me. I won't know until we both return to college.'

'Not getting her phone number was silly.'

James stirred. 'Nor her address. Nor her surname.'

'Yeah, yeah,' Simon said. 'We were having far too much fun for such trivialities.'

'You should have asked her for them,' Imogen said. 'She would've liked it. She would've felt you were interested.'

'Really? Wouldn't she have felt I was kind of annoying?'

'Possibly,' James muttered. 'If she's as weird as you. But who else is?'

Simon took another look through the windows, but there was no sign of Julie or Sarah. He could just about see into the kitchen, where Tim appeared to have an arm around Mary's shoulder. They smoked a joint with Danny.

'Where's Nick?' Simon said.

'He and Heather took themselves away somewhere.' Imogen said.

James grinned drunkenly, his eyes still closed. 'I don't think Mark will sleep in his bed tonight.'

Simon looked around him. 'I think I'd best make sure the rest of the party is still running smoothly. No fights, no arguments.'

'Let's hope you return with a happy Jules,' Imogen said.

Simon stood, and then entered the house through the French windows. He scanned the living room. There had been no new arrivals since Tim and Sarah. Gaz still had control of the record player, and he and Jake were playing air guitar to *Highway Star*. Mark was sitting with Chrissie. She looked as gloomy as she had half-an-hour ago. Various couples were kissing, and friends were sprawled across the floor, drinking and smoking.

Simon went to the hallway where Warren sat chatting on the stairs to Miles and Reese. Warren had been assigned gate guard for this hour. A thought struck Simon. 'Have you seen Nick?' he said.

Warren nodded. 'Last time I saw young Nick, he was heading up these very stairs.' He winked. 'He was with that cracker from Southleigh. Heather?'

'Yes, that's the very girl.'

An empty Party Seven can rolled slowly down the stairs. Will sat on the landing, with somebody else Simon couldn't see. 'Don't do that, you berk. The place will stink of beer.'

'Oh, bugger off, Simon,' somebody said. 'You're too sensible.'

Simon wasn't sure if Will had spoken or if it had been his invisible friend. 'Don't make me come up there,' Simon laughed. Simon looked at Will. He appeared to be very drunk. The party was approaching its danger hour.

Simon went upstairs to see whether anyone had taken over Mark's parent's bedroom. He stepped over Will, and found the unseen friend was Steve. Drunk as they both were, they played canasta. The parent's bedroom was clear. Simon said 'Excuse me,' as he opened other doors. Somebody was in Mark's room, but Simon didn't look too closely. The other rooms, Mark's brother's rooms, were empty. Both brothers had left town, had gone away somewhere, to university, jobs, or something. Simon usually forgot Mark even had brothers. They had never impinged on his life. Simon opened the door to the bathroom. It remained unsullied and unbroken. He returned downstairs. The cloakroom door was locked. 'Are you happy here for a bit longer?' Simon said to Warren. Warren nodded, and then continued chatting to Miles and Reese.

Simon entered the lounge and looked around. The disposition of bodies in chairs and around the floor had changed little. Chrissie and Mark still talked to each other. Chrissie looked grimly at Jake, who was still head-banging with Gaz. Queen now, *Brighton Rock*. Simon walked through the small dining room and then into the kitchen, where he found Mary and Tim kissing. So where was Sarah now? Simon walked out into the back garden. Imo and James remained where he had last seen them. Simon scanned the garden. There was no sign of Sarah, or Julie for that matter.

Simon squatted down next to Imogen. 'Have you seen Julie about?' he said.

'No,' Imogen said. 'Isn't she inside?'

Simon shook his head. 'No. Nor is Sarah. And Tim's now getting off with Mary.'

Imogen looked down at James. His eyes were closed 'Can you help me, Si? James is completely pissed, and my bum has gone to sleep. I need to move.'

Simon slid his arms under James's shoulders, and across the top of Imogen's thighs. 'Pardon me, madam,' he said. He slowly lifted James. 'Come on, old bean.' James muttered something incomprehensible. Simon finally managed to stand James, who leaned heavily against him. Imo stood, bounced on the spot and patted her bottom.

'You go on,' Simon said, 'and make a way. I'll steer this piss-head through to the front door.'

Imogen led Simon and James through the house. 'I'm goin' now,' James mumbled to anybody who could hear. 'Nigh' nigh'. S'bin a pleasure...'

Warren opened the front door. Imogen went through first, out into the hot, dark night. Simon angled James through the door. 'War'n! Miles, Reese. G'night!' James mumbled.

Simon delivered James into Imogen's arms. Luckily, she was a tall girl, and James a short boy. 'Will you be all right?' Simon said.

'This won't be the first time I've manoeuvred a pissed James home. I'll be fine.'

'Where are Kate and Stuart?'

'Either gone home, or still out walking. If you see them, say bye from me.'

'I will.'

'And see you again soon, Si.' Imo kissed his cheek. 'Hope you finally make it with Julie or Anna. Somebody deserves you.'

'Thanks, Imo.'

Imogen steered James around and began walking down the asphalt drive.

'See you, Si,' James mumbled. 'Bye, everyone.'

Simon heard a crash somewhere in the house. He turned. Warren was at the front door, smoking a cigarette. 'Lounge, I think,' Warren said. Simon pushed quickly past him and the others in the hallway. He found Mark on the floor, an overturned table, broken glasses, and Jake bouncing aggressively on his toes. Chrissie sat on the edge of the sofa, gripping the cushions tightly, looking from Mark to Jake.

'You really shouldn't have done that,' Mark said. He held his jaw, which he moved from side to side.

'You shouldn't have called me stupid,' Jake said. 'Just because you think you're smarter than me.'

Mark began to stand. 'I bloody well am smarter than you, you thicko. At least I know how to look after Chrissie.'

Simon moved in between the two of them. There was no doubt this row concerned the dark-haired gamine loved by Mark but dating Jake. Simon also had little doubt that Mark was as much to blame as Jake for all of this. Mark looked drunker than he would normally be. 'I don't know who said what, or who hit who, ' Simon said. 'But this stops here.'

'He hit me,' Mark said.

'You hit me!' Jake said. 'You wanker.'

Jake was pissed, Simon had noticed. He was swaying as he eyed Mark warily. Simon didn't see which of them moved first, but both Jake and Mark went for each other. Simon deflected Jake with his shoulder and then slid his arm under Mark's and allowed Mark's momentum to roll them to the floor.

Simon stared down at a surprised Mark. 'Now, you stay there you idiot.'

Jake had recovered from a drunk-legged turn around the living room, and faced Simon. 'Let me at him.'

Simon slowly stood up. 'How about we calm down and be friends again.'

'Just let me at him,' Jake growled once again.

'Sorry, Jake, but you'll have to go through me.' Simon was aware that not only Jake but the whole party was looking at him. Simon stared at Jake, unflinching, unmoved, adrenaline coursing through his body.

Jake blinked slowly, and wobbled a little. 'Sod it,' he said, 'Mark's really not worth it. None of you are. C'mon Chrissie, let's go.'

Chrissie neither spoke nor moved. Simon thought she might keep the tension simmering by making a grand statement about staying. Finally, she stood. 'All right, then,' she said.

Jake took her hand and led her from the room. The front door slammed. Simon looked down at Mark. 'You can get up now.'

'He's a prat,' Mark said.

'I think *you* should stop drinking,' Simon said. He grabbed Mark's arm and pulled him up from the floor. Stuart and Kate entered the room from the hall. 'What's going on?' Kate said. 'We heard noises.'

'Mark and Jake decided to get feisty,' Simon said, glaring disdainfully at Mark.

Mark slumped onto the sofa. 'I confess I am more than a little tipsy.'

Simon sighed. 'I'll make you a coffee.'

As he passed the French windows, he could hear somebody throwing up in the garden. He looked at his watch. It was one-thirty. There had been a fight, Mark was remorseful, and somebody was puking. Yes, the magic hour had indeed arrived, Simon thought, and smiled ruefully.

Tim stopped kissing Mary. 'So you really can do all that kung fu-ey shit,' he said.

'Yes, I most certainly can,' Simon said.

Mary stroked Tim's cheek and then walked away. Heather was also in the kitchen, wrapped in a sheet. She must have slipped downstairs while Simon had been seeing off James and Imo. She leaned back against a worktop, holding a glass of wine. Simon filled the kettle. He looked at Heather. 'What have you done with Nick?'

'Still upstairs,' Heather said. 'Catching his breath.'

'You're Heather, aren't you,' Tim said.

'I am,' Heather said. 'You should know. I went out with Hobo, and came to The Swan.' She lit a cigarette.

'You're a good-looking girl,' Tim said, slurring.

Heather blew smoke towards the ceiling through pursed lips,

while her eyes smiled. 'I certainly am. And that girl you were kissing... That's Mary. She's my best friend.'

Tim frowned. 'She never said.'

'She was too busy kissing you. I didn't want to interrupt. She seemed to be enjoying your rugged charms. I will certainly *not* step on her toes.'

'Your loss,' said Tim.

'Oh, boo hoo,' said Heather.

The kettle boiled. Simon spooned instant coffee and sugar into a mug. He poured in boiling water. He noticed that Tim was swaying slightly. Well, it was that time of night – the time for swaying and fighting and puking.

'I saw you with Julie,' Tim said. 'Kissing.'

Simon knew that Tim would have to bring it up.

'You kissed Julie?' Heather said. 'Brilliant!'

Tim looked at Heather, wondering, Simon thought, what she was implying, but the result of such concentration merely caused Tim to sway more and frown in confusion. Simon lifted the mug of strong coffee he'd made, ready to carry it through to Mark. Just as he turned, Tim said, 'No, hang on, Si.'

Simon thought for a moment another fight was about to break out, but this time with him at the centre of it. He was poised, ready to throw the coffee in Tim's face. Instead, Tim put his arm around Simon's shoulders. 'You're a good bloke you know, Simon,' he slurred. 'I always said it. You an' all your weird friends. You'd be great for Jules. She misses you all.'

Simon was wrong-footed. 'Well, I, uh, umm...'

'No, mate, you should go for it. I'm all wrong for her, I think. She needs all her old friends.'

'So what's going on with Sarah? That really pissed of Jules. Where's she gone?'

'Oh, that? That was nothing. Sarah jus' needed a friend to come to the party with her. Wasn't like it looked. I really like Mary.' At that moment, Mary returned. 'There you are. We should go to my place.' Tim was old enough to have his own flat. Simon envied him that. Mary whispered in Tim's ear. He raised an eyebrow, and smirked. 'All right! Night, Simon. You look after Jules.'

'Uh, yes, I will. Night, Tim. Goodnight Mary.'

Mary went to Heather and kissed her cheek. She whispered something to Heather, and then turned back Tim. They left then, arm in arm. Simon remained where he was.

'You look discombobulated,' Heather said.

'Well, I didn't expect that,' Simon said.

'Me neither. I was looking forward to a proper punch-up. I never liked Tim.'

Will entered the kitchen, looking greener than the leaves had been for the last few months. He nodded most abjectly at Simon.

Simon went back into the lounge. There were fewer bodies around. People had begun to drift away. Gaz was still by the record deck, spinning quieter music now. It sounded like something by Mike Oldfield. *Ommadawn*, perhaps. Mark was a fan. He still sat on the sofa, looking glum. Simon thought it best to leave him that way. He gave Mark his coffee, and then began picking up plastic cups and paper plates.

Warren was leaving. He found Simon to say goodnight. Simon followed him to the door. Warren said the party had been great fun, and that the best bit by far was the fight, even though it had been over far too quickly. Simon opened the front door for Warren, and was surprised to find Julie there, her arm raised, about to ring the doorbell.

'Hi, Jules,' Warren said. 'You're not here to walk me home, are you?'

'You're quite right,' Julie said.

Warren gave a wave and walked off down the drive.

'I'm here–' Julie began, but then Heather came into the hall and interrupted her.

'Hey, Julie! You came back! Good to see you!' Heather ran up the stairs, a ghost in her sheet. 'Shame you missed the fight, Julie,' she called out.

'A fight?' Julie said. She frowned at Simon. 'I hope it wasn't between you and Tim.'

'Oh no, not me and Tim. Come on, come inside,' Simon said. He told her about Jake and Mark.

'They'll get over it,' Julie said. 'Chrissie'll make sure of that. They'll soon be friends again.'

'I'm pleasantly surprised to see you. I thought I'd lost you for the night.'

'I had to talk to Sarah about Tim. We went for a walk. She said there was nothing between her and Tim. She needed an escort for the party. She doesn't know you lot as well as I do.'

'Yes, that's what Tim said.'

'So, where is he now? I really need to have a word with him.'

'He's gone home.' Simon looked at Julie, and wondered what she was thinking, what she was feeling. 'He went home with Mary. A while ago.'

Julie looked at Simon, wide-eyed. 'Mary? You mean, Heather's scary friend? *That* Mary?'

'Yes, *that* Mary. So you came back for Tim?' Simon said. He was disappointed now. Things with Julie felt different again. He had so enjoyed the earlier part of this evening. To not kiss her, to not hold her, was a cold blast of reality on a night that remained still and sultry.

'I came back to find you. And my bag,' Julie said. 'But mainly you.'

Simon's stomach fluttered then. He felt light.

'I do need to speak to Tim,' Julie said. 'If he'd been here, I could've got that done.'

Simon couldn't begin to imagine why Julie felt the need to talk to Tim.

'I really want to apologise, though,' Julie said. 'For leaving you like that. We were having fun, weren't we?'

Simon noticed the question. He discerned the insecurity that lay behind it. He put his arms around her. 'Yes, we were.'

'Yes, we were,' Julie repeated softly. She kissed him, and then

104

relaxed into his arms. 'But I do need to go home. I'm tired. And I'm almost certainly still drunk.'

'I'll walk you home, if you like, ' Simon said.

'Of *course* I'd like that,' Julie said.

Julie began to search for her bag. Simon surveyed what was left of the party, the revenants and remnants that remained. Most of the party-goers had left now. Mark remained slumped and glum on the sofa. Gaz had crashed out on the floor beside the record player, from which something quietly played. Steve and Will had moved their canasta game from the landing to the lounge. Steve said that they were playing to one hundred thousand, and it might take until morning to finish. Will said he had seen Kate and Stuart go heading to a bedroom upstairs.

Simon went over to the forlorn Mark. 'I'm walking Julie home, but I'll be back. Don't start any more fights.'

'It wasn't me,' Mark began. 'It was that–'

'Let me stop you right there. I don't care.'

Simon and Julie walked up Barton Road slowly, drugged by the heat, somnolent. They held hands as they walked. They passed jasmine that sweetly scented the still, sticky night.

Simon squeezed Julie's hand. 'I had fun, Jules.'

Simon's hand was squeezed in return. 'So did I.'

'And you and Sarah sorted it all out?'

'Yes, we did.'

They walked quietly for a while. Julie put her head on Simon's shoulder. Simon stopped, pulled Julie to him, and kissed her.

'You're lovely,' Julie said.

'Lovely enough?' Simon asked, although he wasn't sure why.

'Lovely enough.'

Simon wasn't sure what Julie meant. They kissed again though, before resuming their walk back to Julie's house.

'I forget about Anna when we kiss,' Simon said.

'Is that good?' Julie wondered.

'I think so.'

Julie gently nudged him with her shoulder. 'Oh, you're so passionate,' she said.

Simon laughed. 'But I do like kissing you.'

They talked as they walked, about Mark and Jake, about Chrissie, Nick and Heather, and Sarah.

At the door to the house, Simon took Julie in his arms again. 'I really enjoyed this evening,' he said. 'The early part. The bit with you in it.'

Julie looked into his eyes. 'I did, too.'

'Really?'

'You'd better believe it, Simon.' Julie lifted her face and found Simon's lips. He melted once again into her kiss. Their tongues touched, and Simon thought that, perhaps, everything might be all right, that something might grow out of all this, that this summer would now be full of sweet scents and kisses.

Julie broke the kiss, and then leaned her forehead against Simon's. She touched his cheek. 'This is so lovely, Si.' She closed her eyes. 'So, so lovely', she whispered again. 'But I'm so confused.' She kissed his cheek, then turned and pushed her key into the lock. 'Look, I'll see you, soon, yeah?' Julie said softly.

Though Simon was now also confused, he said, 'Yeah, of course you will. We could meet tomorrow.'

That won a wide, warm smile from Julie. 'That would be great,' she said. She kissed Simon on the cheek once again, and entered the house.

Simon turned and walked down the short driveway, through the gate and onto Town Road. He looked at his watch. It was two in the morning. He headed back towards Mark's house, to check that it and Mark had survived the party.

The warm breeze carried other garden scents, honeysuckle, night-scented stock, Simon didn't know what else. The breeze lifted from his shoulder, the shoulder on which Julie's cheek had so often rested, a memento from Julie – the scent of Charlie, or Tramp, or something. *King Arthur's Avalon.* He smiled. He walked slowly back to Mark's. He recalled one moment in particular – a long honeyed kiss as he and Julie danced to *Make it With You*. He was overwhelmed then with a medley of memories – the ghost of Julie in his arms, her perfume, the peasant skirt, kisses, blonde hair, bright eyes. He sighed. He had no idea what tomorrow would bring. Rather than become caught up in what-ifs and what-nexts, Simon thought it better to carry down the dark, dusty, road only those memories, only those images, only those feelings from the best parts of this evening. This might be, after all, as good as it ever gets.

I may be climbing on rainbows, but baby...

Walking

7

This is You

PAGE of CUPS.

Julie had woken mid-morning with only a mild headache. She showered, ate some toast, and swallowed three aspirins with her sweet coffee. She lit a cigarette, and then went to the phone, and rang Simon's house. His mother answered, and said he had popped in for breakfast, but then gone back to help out Mark. Julie said thank you, and replaced the handset. She went to the table to finish her breakfast, her coffee and the cigarette. The house was empty but for her. Her mum and dad usually went to her gran's for their Sunday lunch, and it seemed that her sister had also gone out.

It was another hot day in this long hot, dry, dusty summer. The sky was again unclouded, a brilliant blue, the sun fierce.

She tapped her cigarette on the thick glass ash-tray on the table. She was still half-asleep. Her thoughts returned to last night, to kissing, to hugging and dancing, to laughing and smiling and warmth. All of these things were very good. But still, beneath it all, there lay confusion, and something clouding this sunny day. What could it be? Could it be that she still loved Tim? Was love so irrational that despite everything that had happened last night, despite enjoying the kisses and being with Simon's friends, she could still wonder if she'd made a mistake?

Today, though, she wanted Simon. She decided to walk around to Mark's and see if he was still there. Even if he wasn't, she could ask Mark if he had said anything about her, even though she knew this was silly when she was still uncertain about Tim, but still she wanted to know – and needed to know – that Simon fancied *her*, that he liked her more than Anna and Imo and anybody else. She wanted to be the centre of his world, selfish as that might be. She wanted to be loved. But then, who didn't?

She needed to get dressed. She still wore the light dressing gown over the underwear she had put on when she had come out of the shower. She went upstairs to find some clothes. In her room she took off the gown and caught sight of herself in the full-length mirror. She thought she'd put on weight. She turned then and looked at her bottom. She shook her head. She was being stupid. Hadn't Simon just spent all night kissing her? He *did* fancy her. Although, given that he was so shy, he might never actually say anything or do anything beyond kiss her at parties. Yet it would be nice to hang out with Simon, even if he never moved beyond kissing and holding hands and looking at her hopefully and most awkwardly. But there was the Anna thing. His Anna thing might be different to her Tim thing, but it certainly added to the confusion they both felt.

The only thing to do was *enjoy*. Love the one you're with, as Stephen Stills once sang. This summer was far too fabulous to do otherwise. She would lay back, chill-out, remain relaxed through these dreamy, hazy, lazy days. Because – no matter what happened – Simon and sunshine, walks across hills, hot nights, hands, lips, dancing, smiles, and car rides with the wind in her hair would be *this* hot summer for ever now, and this summer would always be the perfect summer that no future summer could ever equal.

She pulled on an old pair of jeans, a scoop-neck tee-shirt and pink boots, then went back down to the kitchen where she picked up her cigarettes, lighter, and her purse. She left the house and walked along Barton Road towards Mark's house. She hoped Simon would still be there, even if she was unsure what it was she wanted with him. One thing she could do with Simon, she had learned, was *relax*. He made that easy. She crossed the road at Goldfinch Drive and glanced up it, but there was no Simon. There was nobody on the dusty roads this hot morning.

She smoked as she walked, squinting at the sky, breathing out thin clouds that mimicked the high white wisps of cirrus. She was confused, but happy. She could imagine ending this summer back with Tim, but would that be right? She remembered what she'd been thinking a few days ago – that Tim appeared more dynamic than Simon, that she imagined doing more kinds of things with Tim, and how those things might be more exciting than anything she did with the laid-back Simon and all his friends. Yet those friends were fun in other ways, and offered other diversions – Honeyhouse, a world of music and all the excitement that involved, and The Prophets, and their world of reading, walking, talking, films and theatre and galleries. Romantic with a capital R. She remembered what she had called Simon; a decadent aesthete. She liked that. It was better than *the Prophets*. They weren't *all* decadent. Simon was rather clean living for a young guy – tai chi, of course, and kung fu interested him most. But James was drifting into decadence, what with all the drinking, and Danny too, with the drugs.

She reached Mark's house and turned into the driveway. where she dropped her cigarette and crushed it beneath her boot, and then approached the front door. She found it open. She poked her head around the door, and was about to call out when Simon came quickly down the stairs.

'Water! Water! Nick is on fire,' he called out as he reached the hallway. He saw Julie. 'Jules! Come on in. We're tidying. We've nearly finished.'

Julie put her arms around Simon. 'Good morning. What's happened to Nick?'

Simon kissed her forehead. 'He says he's on fire. He's burning up.' He led her into the now shipshape front room.

'Is he still in bed with Heather?'

'He is.'

'Still?'

'Indeed. But I think they're getting ready to move out. They're now under pressure from Mark. It'll be the last room tidied.'

'How is it?'

'From my brief visit, it smells of cigarettes, drink, sweat, patchouli and something I can only yet imagine is sex. There are glasses everywhere, the ashtrays are full, and all the sheets and blankets – except the ones Heather and Nick wrap themselves in when they bless us with their presence – are on the floor. It's a scene of filth, dereliction and decay.'

Julie laughed at Simon's description. 'How would you know what sex smells like?'

'Guesswork. I eliminated all the known scents, smells and odours. What remained was the still unknown. And as you kindly pointed out, that kind of sex is still unknown to me. QED.'

'What? Only *that* kind?'

'Indeed, all kinds, as well you know. I am, after all, the shy boy.'

'Yes, I know,' Julie said. 'Don't be ashamed of it. I rather like it.'

'Oh, I'm not. I'll know when I'm ready for *that*.' They had reached the kitchen. Simon found a glass and filled it from the tap. He looked at Julie with a warm, open smile. 'Back in a moment.' He walked quickly out of the kitchen towards the hallway and the stairs.

Julie looked out of the window, into the sun-drenched back garden. Mark and Gaz were out there in the heat, picking up drink cans and bottles and placing them in stacks and heaps. She found the kettle and filled it, then switched it on. She wondered if Simon wanted sex with her, had wanted to have sex with her last night. Although she had indeed enjoyed kissing Simon, and Simon had seemed to enjoy kissing her, there had been, somehow, something chaste about it, something sexless. That had been part of the pleasure of last night, and partly why it was already in the process of becoming a memory to cherish on less sunny days. Simon's innocent unknowing led to a kind of passionate but sexless embrace. For Julie, the absence of any *desire* at the party was a throwback to how it had been when initiated in the art of kissing at about twelve years old. As she grew older, boys had become much more forceful - kissing had become the prelude to everything else, even when she herself wished kissing to be the only thing. Simon provided something else - adult kissing and adult arms, an adult knowing; yet no force. She had never felt the kissing last night would lead somewhere she had no interest in yet visiting. There had been only kissing. How could she explain Simon's soft, warm but desire-less kissing, and why she had so enjoyed it, to somebody like Tim.

The kettle boiled. Julie made coffee for her and Simon. He returned from his errand. He looked happy. Julie handed Simon a mug. 'What are you grinning about?'

Simon shrugged. His eyes sparkled 'Just... everything. Nick said something vaguely amusing. And you're here. And the sun continues to shine.' He looked through the kitchen window. 'Even Gaz and Mark have charmed me this morning. Today's a good day.' He looked at Julie as he sipped his coffee, and then said to her, 'Even if you don't know what you want.'

'Oh! Sorry, Simon,' Julie said.

Simon smiled. 'Don't worry. I'm just being a bit cheeky. What's happening now is... well, *fun*. Whatever happens with us next...' He finished uncertainly. He looked at her, into her eyes. 'Well, we'll always have Paris.'

Julie laughed. She knew the reference – she'd seen *Casablanca* often enough.

Mark came into the kitchen, sweating, and pulled opened the fridge. 'Good lord, it's hot out there,' he said. He took out two cans of cola. He ripped the ring-pull from one can and took a slug. Some cola ran down his chin. 'We've nearly finished,' he said. 'You don't have to be here.' He took another swig. 'I'm going to crash out when we've finished.'

Julie looked at Simon. 'Do you fancy a walk?' She said. 'With me?'

'Oh, yes please,' Simon said. 'Although I'm not sure I've got the energy to make it up Copsehill today.'

'You two should go south for a change,' Mark said. 'I was only thinking the other day that we hardly ever go out south of the town. So I took a look at the maps. There's plenty of footpaths out there. Hang on...' Mark went to the front room, and came back with the OS map.

'Thanks, man,' Simon said. 'Great idea.'

'I'm returning to the garden. Gaz will wonder where his drink's gone.'

Simon finished his coffee and then rinsed his mug. Julie swigged hers down. Simon took her mug and rinsed it.

'Thank you,' Julie said.

'Shall we go?' Simon said.

Julie nodded. 'Let's.'

They bumped into Heather and Nick in the hallway. Despite a night of drink and sex and little sleep, Heather still looked good. Julie envied her.

'Si! Jules!' Nick said. 'Are you going?'

'Yes. We're off for a walk,' Simon said. Julie noted that he didn't suggest Nick and Heather join them. She took Simon's hand and laced her fingers through his.

'We couldn't join you even if you wanted us to,' Nick said, and winked. 'We're completely knackered. We need some coffee and a plan to get Heather back to Southleigh.'

'See you down the Lion later,' Simon said.

'Thank you for all your help,' Heather said. 'I don't know how we would have made it through the night without you.'

'Although,' Nick said, 'you didn't need to stand outside the door shouting *Come on, team, keep pushing.*'

They laughed, and then Simon opened the front door and led Julie into the sun. It was very hot, and Julie wondered if walking was a good idea. Still, she wanted to be alone with Simon. She knew that each day might be their last day together, and she didn't want to waste a day. One day it would rain, a long grey, slow rain, and the whole atmosphere of this summer would at last change.

They had no need of Mark's map yet. They wandered along Barton Road, and then turned into Goldfinch Drive. They were heading to Simon's house where they picked up some cans of drink, which Simon put into his faded blue knapsack along with the map Mark had given to him. Simon's mother said they should take some food, and gave them custard creams. She also said they needed hats, otherwise they would get sunstroke. She found a trilby for Simon, and an outback hat for Julie. 'Here, put these on,' she said. They did. Then they laughed and swapped them over, so that Julie had the trilby.

'That's more stylish,' Simon's mum said.

Simon slung the knapsack over his head and shoulder, and then they left the house and walked along Magpie Road out of the estate, towards the fields to the south-west. They talked about the last night again, especially about Nick and Heather, and the fight.'

'And you're cool about Sarah now?' Simon asked.

'Oh, yes. Yes, we're fine. We sorted it all out last night.'

'You've been friends with her since you were about six years old, haven't you?'

'Something like that. We first met when we started at primary school.'

They were out in the fields now, heading along a well-worn path across the yellow and brown grass. Julie squinted into the sunlight, towards a stand of trees ahead. The path went through a copse she knew was called the Blue Ball. She had no idea why it should be called that.

Julie bit her lip, and then said, as casually as she could. 'So, what have our friends said about us?'

Simon put an arm around her. 'Gaz was he usual subtle self.'

'I can imagine,' Julie laughed. 'Please don't tell me what *he* said.'

Simon nodded his head. 'Very wise. Mark... well actually he didn't say much. He did say we looked as though we were enjoying ourselves quite a lot.'

'I was,' Julie said.

'So was I.' Simon said. He squeezed her to him. Julie liked it.

They were quiet for a moment. She looked at Simon. He smiled back.

'I liked what Imogen said best,' he finally said.

'Oh, really?' Julie said. 'So what did she say?'

'She said we looked good together. She said we looked most *genial*.'

'Genial,' Julie said quietly. 'Trust Imo to think of that word.' She felt a warmth growing inside. 'Hah! Genial,' she said again. 'How lovely.' She kissed Simon's cheek.

They reached the shade of the Blue Ball. The way narrowed as it entered the stand of trees between the trunks, and brambles and ferns now crowded across the dusty path. Simon took his arm from Julie's shoulders, and trod a path into the copse.

'I so need a drink,' Julie said.

Simon removed a bottle of fizzy drink from his haversack and passed it over to Julie. She unscrewed the top and swigged down some of the fizzy, warm orange. She passed the bottle to Simon. He gulped some down and offered the bottle back. Julie shook her head and Simon returned it to his bag. It was cooler under the trees, and smelled of the dust on the paths, and of the dry leaves on the ferns and brambles, and of the dry wood.

'Glad I have this hat,' Julie said. 'I think your mum is very wise.'

'She might be. Sometimes,' Simon said.

'So, how do I look?' Julie said. She tilted her hat from behind, then touched her thumb and finger to the brim like a Fosse dancer.

'Perfectly lovely,' Simon said. He came across to her, and kissed her cheek, then looked for a moment into her eyes. His blue eyes were so soft today, reflecting hers. He held the look. He was asking her a question, Julie realised. Then he kissed her, gently, on her lips. He was still trying to find out where their boundaries were, which of the paths he could follow; but she also had no idea where they might be, or where they led. Simon turned, looked around the copse. 'We should consult the map.' he said.

Julie nodded. 'Where shall we go?'

Simon looked at her. 'Who knows, Jules?' The question was still in his eyes, but his look was playful.

They knew the way out of the copse; they had both walked this path before. Later in the walk things would become a little more uncertain. They both knew the downs and the Plain to the north of the town better than this wide and shallow vale. Simon opened the map, turned it around several times, folded various flaps in various ways, until he was happy he had sufficient map in view to guide them through the next hour or two.

Julie found The Blue Ball on the map before Simon even

pointed. 'This is where we are,' Simon said. Even on the map, the copse looked almost perfectly circular.

'Look. There's another path out of here,' Julie said.

'Yes, I see that too. Well, I never knew that before.'

They both looked up, across the copse. The path was little used, Julie saw. There was only a hint of its exit through the trees. She looked back at the map. The path headed out the copse directly to the south across a field, and then into another field.

Simon had already scouted ahead. 'Look,' he said, pointing into the map. 'Hammersmith. *In ruins.* It must be an old deserted village.'

'I think my dad may have said something about it once.'

'I've never heard of it. I really must buy some maps.'

'Then we could explore together,' Julie said.

'Oh, absolutely.'

Simon stood, and helped Julie up. As she stood she walked into his arms. 'Yes, let's explore some more,' she said quietly, and kissed his neck.

They turned and walked through undergrowth maculate with the dappled sun that pierced the curled brown leaves. As they walked they kicked up dust from the ground, and brushed against the dusty leaves of nettles and ground ivy. Julie stopped and looked across the copse. Motes floated through rays of sunshine. She turned and caught up with Simon. When they reached the barely-limned path, Simon went first, pressing down the brambles and nettles with his boots. Once outside of the copse Julie could barely see the line of the path as it continued across desiccated brown pasture.

Julie stopped and shielded her eyes against the sun. She could see a stile in the distant fence. She skipped back alongside Simon and threaded an arm through his. 'I do wonder what happened with Tim and that Mary,' she said.

'Do you *really* care?' Simon said.

'I can't help but wonder,' Julie said.

'To be honest, I wonder as well. All I know is that they left the party together. Do you think she really went back to his place?'

'Probably. Tim isn't backwards at coming forward.' She glanced up at Simon then, unsure how he would handle that information. He was squinting towards the stile, as serenely *Simon* as ever.

When they reached the stile, they found two footpath signs, one pointing south-west, the other south-east. They climbed up onto the stile, sat on the top wooden bar, and consulted the map.

'The path forks here,' Simon said. 'I wonder which way we should go?'

Julie looked out across the field. The south-east path was even fainter than the path they had already walked.

'We should take the path least travelled.'

Simon squinted along each path. 'It *is* grassy and wanting wear.'

'Frost-y,' Julie said.

'Very droll,' Simon looked at the map again. 'The right-hand fork goes on to Southleigh, via Up the Leg.'

'And Down the Stocking, ' Julie finished.

'Indeed. It's a weird kind of name. Who comes up with them?'

'Tradition? I think it's always been favoured by courting couples.'

'Just as well we're not heading that way.'

Everything Simon said today seemed to have a double meaning. Julie kissed his cheek, anyway. They walked down the treads of the stile and began to follow the path less-travelled. It headed quickly across the field, where they climbed yet another stile, and then followed a whitethorn hedge in which beech trees stood. The field was filled with shining barley.

'I'm not sure I care anyway,' Julie said.

Simon looked at her. 'What about?'

'Tim and Mary, and Tim in general.'

'*That* conundrum.'

'Yes, that.'

'Perhaps he'll go out with her. It might make things clearer if he did.'

'Perhaps.'

The path between the hedge and the crop was narrow. Julie followed Simon, holding onto his hand. She couldn't see Simon's face. 'What about you?'

'Me?'

'You and Anna.'

'At the moment, I think you and Tim are the problem. Until you can see past all that I don't know. There's you and there's me, and then there's Tim and there's Anna.' Simon shrugged 'It's... intricate.' He stopped walking, and turned to face her. 'We should just enjoy this. Whatever this is.'

Julie nodded, and then they held each other in the dreaming heat. When they broke apart, they walked to the corner of the field and stopped under the shade of a tall beech. They drank some more warm orangeade. Simon studied the map again. In the hedge was another stile. Julie removed her hat and fanned herself with it.

'We cross this stile,' Simon said. 'Then we're in South Field. There's a row of trees to walk through, and then we finally reach Hammersmith.'

Julie looked back the way they had come. She could see the ridgelines and chimney pots of Dereham in the hazed and shimmering distance. They climbed the stile, and began to walk again. She took the map from Simon. She could see the paths they had followed marked in dashed lines across it. She looked around her. So many of the features placed on the map by the map-makers were still here, barns and ponds and clumps. The map showed a building ahead.

'There should be barn,' Julie said. 'Baxter's Bake Barn.' She stopped and, shielding her eyes against the sun's glare, looked ahead. 'There's nothing there now.'

'*Do* remember... The map is not the territory,' Simon said.

'Wow, man, ' Julie said. '*Intense.*'

'You've heard that one before, haven't you.'

'Yes. Bloody hippies,' Julie said.

As they approached the gate, Julie could see lumps and bumps in the grass where the map had shown the barn should be. She walked over, and looked at the ground. Simon followed. She could see in the grass masonry and brick, scattered, as if the building had tumbled down. She looked around her. A spine of old stones, white and grey, cemented with crumbling, yellow lime, pushed its vertebrae through the grass.

Simon opened the gate in the hedge and he and Julie walked through it.

'We're here,' Julie said. 'Hammersmith.'

The path took them between nettles, rosebay willowherb, brambles and ivy. Walls had tumbled beside the track. Julie could see the ghosts of gardens, and walls, and paddocks. 'So when was all this abandoned?'

Simon shook his head. 'I don't know. I didn't know about it. We should look it up... Somewhere.'

'We could visit the library,' Julie said. She wanted to know more about this place. 'They'll have books.'

'What's that?' Simon pointed to a building that was larger than the others, its walls almost intact. They pushed through a broken black gate. Simon stopped, and looked down. 'Hey, Jules! It's a headstone.'

Julie walked over. 'A graveyard?' She looked at the building again, and then down at the map. There was a cross drawn where they stood.

'Look,' here,' she said, pointing and then handing the map back to Simon. 'It's an old church. St Leonard's.'

The church was small, little more than a box with no roof, and no timbers left that could begin to show the shape and size of it. They walked along beside one of the grey stone walls. Even though there was no roof, the windows were boarded, the door locked.

'It must be deconsecrated,' Simon said. 'Otherwise it would be in better shape. Not this mess.'

At the rear of the building, arches curved above them, arches that had once supported something, but now supported only the branches of trees and the blue sky above them. Julie found a faded sign on one of the pillars, warning that the building was dangerous. Through the arches, pictures changed and moved: branches swayed, clouds drifted, small birds flashed by, leaves whispered and danced.

'How interesting,' Julie said quietly. She took Simon's hand. 'And you've never been here before?'

'No,' Simon said. 'I don't walk out this way very often. And if I do, I take the other path.'

'Up the Leg and Down the Stocking?'

'Is that an offer?'

Julie smiled. 'Not today, Si.'

Simon pouted. 'Well, when you're me, you do need to check you haven't missed a signal.'

'Everything we've done this summer, and everything we do now, is *perfect*.'

'Yes, it is,' Simon said. He ran his hand under her hair and around the back of her neck. A shiver ran down Julie's spine. She closed her eyes. She knew Simon understood.

He gently pulled her along with him. She opened her eyes as they passed beneath an arch. 'In and out the dusty windows.'

'It's bluebells,' Simon said.

'It's *what*?'

'In and out the dusty bluebells.'

'No, it's windows.'

'No, it's bluebells.'

They walked around the other side of the broken church to the path.

'How often did you sing *In and Out the Dusty Windows*?' Julie said.

'Never. Because it's *In and Out the Dusty Bluebells*. At least, that's what the girls sang at my school.'

'We sang *windows*. And we were right.'

'You were not.'

'We bloody well were.'

'Is this our first big argument?'

'Shall we get divorced?'

'Not until we're married, at the very least.'

The path still headed south, past overgrown gardens and plots. Simon took the map from his bag and studied it again. He found another bottle of orangeade and offered it to Julie. He looked around at the houses, overgrown gardens and trees. 'The track we came down goes through the village. At the end of the village it becomes Gypsy Lane,' Simon said. 'The field next to it has a name. Glebe Field.'

Julie returned the drink. 'I suppose every field was named in those days,' she said. 'People worked on the land, and had to know which field to go to. *Glebe*. Funny word.'

'And if you had to tell someone which field to go to, you might have to tell them which road to walk down. I suppose every road and path and lane had a name.'

'Arr,' Julie said, exaggerating her Wiltshire accent. 'Take thic path, they'd say, Poppy Lane, thee knows it?'

'You be roight,' Simon added. 'Then over Glebe Field and down Shap's Path to White Scar Hanging, you see the ripples on the downs?'

'Oi do, sir. And that'll be the path at the bottom, Gypsy Lane, follow that to Green Field. Arr, that'll see thee roight, it will.'

'Thank ee, ma'am,' Simon said, and touched the brim of his hat. 'Oi'll be getting along then, now. Heel, Shep.'

'Don't call me Shep. I'm no dog.'

'Sorry. Come on then, me lovely.'

As they were about to walk out into fields bathed in bright sunlight framed in the curving branches of beech and alder,

Simon slowed. He looked to his left. Julie turned. There was another building there. Like the other buildings they had seen, it had no roof, and no door. Only the brown, worm-holed remnants of one rotting wooden frame remained. Simon and Julie pushed their way through brambles and nettles to the house. It contained only two rooms, now. The first room they entered was open to the sky. There were oddments scattered about the ground, among the docks and thistles and low shrubs; a few odd knick-knacks, broken remnants of the lives of former inhabitants. A rusting boot-scraper that must once have stood outside; an old table, worm-eaten, three-legged, tilting drunkenly; stairs to nowhere. Only fragments of material – green, red, wool, cord – remained on the stairs. The paint flaked and bubbled on the damp walls, revealing coats of many colours, reds and umbers and blues and greens. In the back room, layers of wallpaper peeled away, the passage of time marked by changing designs – colours bold and colours pastel, floral patterns and abstract patterns. The sagging ceiling remained almost in place. The crumbling lime and horse-hair daub disclosed the latticework of laths that had once held it.

'Do you think this was the last house to be abandoned?' Julie said.

'Yes, it could have been,' Simon said. 'I wonder when, though? And why?'

There was something sad about the house, the way it sagged and flaked, the way the stairs climbed to a bedroom and bed that were no longer there. Who had lived here? Had they been happy? Were there children and games, a front garden full of pansies and roses and tulips, and a back garden with potatoes, lettuce and shallots?

They returned to the room they had first entered. It had only two and a half walls. The most complete wall was that containing the chimney. The breast and flue was a buttress that had helped the wall remain standing. The stack above the roof line that would have held the pot had long gone, now a pile of broken bricks that had tumbled inside the walls. It had fallen a long time ago – the bricks were covered in weeds. Julie kicked back some brambles and found broken grey slate tiles. She flattened more of the weeds, wondering what else she might find. Some beer cans, unsurprisingly; crisp packets, a glass Coke bottle. So other people still used this path. She found a picture frame, face down. She picked it up, wondering what was in it.

The glass had long since broken, but the frame held a damp, faded photograph – of what, though, she wasn't sure. The photo had been printed on thick paper. Areas of faded black and grey remained. Julie could make out a coat, fragments of trees, some grass, and a river, perhaps. There was enough of a head to guess by the hairstyle that there was at least one woman here. There was an eye, a fragment of mouth, a nose, and a shoulder. Would the eye have been blue or brown? There was no way of knowing. Julie imagined big brown eyes. Though the glass had gone, and the photo had faded and was flaking, devoured slowly by chucky pigs and silverfish, the back of the frame remained. Julie tried to pull the picture out from the front, but time had somehow glued the paper to the wooden frame. She didn't want to rip the picture from the frame and ruin it. To do so would be wrong. She managed to prise off the back and revealed water-stained paper. There was a signature, a message, in ink that had run but remained legible.

> *Maggie, you are still beautiful. You will always be beautiful. Be mine again, always. Richard.*

'Si, look at this,' Julie called out.

Simon came over. She gave him the photograph. He looked at it and then turned it over. He smiled.

'Do you think Maggie was ever Richard's again?' Julie wondered.

'Or was he spurned?' Simon said. 'Did Maggie marry someone else? Was Richard for ever alone, forlorn?' '

Julie took the photograph back. 'Oh, I really hope not,' she said. She looked again at the photo and then around her, at the ruins, at these fragments of a person, and of a life. She walked over to one of the rotting window frames. She found what she was looking for; a small nail, a pin really, that was secured old beading. She pulled it easily from the rotten wood. She went to the old fireplace, where she pushed the pin through the photo and into the soft lime mortar between the bricks in the wall above where the mantelpiece would once have been. She stepped backwards.

Simon came and stood next to her. 'Maggie's where she should be,' he said.

Julie held Simon's hand. 'Yes, she is.'

8

This is Your Environment

Simon and Julie had been out for a walk on another still, unclouded day, and were coming into town on one of the lanes that was a twisting way to Southleigh. As they passed the cricket ground, Simon stopped to watch the local club team playing there. He leaned against a low brick wall. Julie wandered on for a moment, and then stopped when she realised he had, and came back. She looked over the wall at the game.

'I've never really understood cricket,' Julie said.

'Nobody has,' Simon said.

Simon entered into that slow world where action is compressed into small frenetic quanta of activity – whirling arms and flailing bats, the sound of the ball on willow, a smattering of applause, white figures sprinting across the brown grass.

Julie lit a cigarette. 'It's a bit boring, isn't it,' she said.

'Slow,' Simon said. 'That's what you mean to say. It has quiet, slow rhythms.'

'Boring would be another way of putting it.'

Lazy bees flew by them to the knapweed and scabious growing at the field's edge. The batsman played a fine late cut. Simon applauded.

'Why are you clapping?' Julie said, blowing smoke into the sky, the only clouds there.

'It was a lovely shot,' Simon said. 'Classy.'

'It looked like a man hitting a ball with a plank.'

'Heathen,' Simon said.

Julie pulled Simon towards town. 'Come along, Simon. I want a drink. I very much *need* a drink.'

Six days had passed since the walk to Hammersmith. There had been fewer kisses and hugs over that time. They had seen each other less often, but there was more to it than that. Simon knew that Julie still wondered what to do about Tim, and thought she would return to him in time. Perhaps when this languid, shining, blue and yellow summer was over, when the sun had set one last time on an unhurried, golden evening, and the sultry, brilliant, rainless, cloudless days had darkened and come to a cold, grey close, then their shared dream would also end and they would become again the people they had been a few weeks ago. Simon. Julie. There would no more be geniality. There would be no more Simon *and* Julie.

They reached The White Lion. A gust of wind lifted the dust in the Market Place. Julie led Simon up the steps and into the saloon bar. Mark was there, sitting with Gray and Chris. The bar was empty but for these three. It was still early in the evening. Simon was pleased to see they had drinks already. He couldn't afford to stand a round, and would barely be able to buy a drink for both himself and Julie. Simon bought Julie a cold lemonade. It was all she wanted after their long hot walk. Simon decided on a lemonade, lime, soda water and ice. He carried the drinks across to the table where their friends sat.

'Hello,' Chris said.

'How's the car?' Simon asked, as he sat.

'We're waiting on a few parts,' Chris said. 'It was a bigger job than I thought.'

'And I haven't had a car for ages,' Gray said. 'All this walking is exhausting. I'll be an old, old man way before my time.'

'It'll be good for you,' Julie said. She took a cigarette offered by Mark.

Gray pouted. 'But it's too hot to walk.'

'We've been exploring,' Simon said. 'Down south.'

'So everybody's been saying.' Gray said.

'What?' Simon said. 'Oh, I see. Very droll.'

'No,' Julie said. 'We've been walking. It's lovely.'

'So you haven't,' Mark said, with a glint in his eye, 'let Simon explore the local hills and valleys, then?'

Julie blushed a little. 'Never you mind who's been exploring what and where. Simon is a gentleman explorer, anyway.'

Simon wondered if he should have explored more while the territory was still open to him. But he also knew he had no idea how to begin such exploration; if any such exploration had been invited or desired, he would have needed Julie as guide to her domains.

'Mark gave us his map of the south,' Simon said.

'Hah!' Chris said. 'That would truly be a map to an imaginary territory.'

'Oh, do piss off you cheeky sod,' Mark said.

'What's happening tonight?' Julie asked. 'I need to go home after this drink and get a bite to eat. Are we here later?'

'Some of us will be,' Mark said. 'Others will be at Copsehill.'

'What's happening up there?'

'The Prophets are going to commune with... Well, with

something. Paul's up from Devon for the weekend. He and James are going to do an occult ritual to get in contact with a spirit... or something of that nature.'

Julie's sighed. 'Please tell me Imogen is too sensible to go along with this.'

'I think Imo's only going with them to make sure James doesn't cause any mischief.'

'They're still together, then,' Simon said.

'Yes. And Kate will be there too, with Stuart.'

'Charlie?' Simon said.

'Yes. He'll also be there.'

Simon hadn't seen Charlie around lately. He still had a Yes album he'd borrowed from Charlie, and which he must give back soon.

'There'll be drugs involved,' Julie said. 'I know it. And Imo will be annoyed with James again.'

'Let's hope they don't let loose an angry fiend from another dimension,' Simon said.

'It must have happened once before,' Gray said.

'What? Why do you say that?' Julie asked.

'It's the only explanation for Gaz.'

They laughed.

'Well, I'm not joining them,' Julie said.

'Nor us,' Chris said. 'We'll be down here later.'

'So, we'll see you here, then,' Simon said.

Simon and Julie finished their drinks. 'I need to go,' Julie said. 'I'm hungry.'

'I'll walk some more with you,' Simon said.

'Don't go exploring,' Gray said, 'in the streets.'

'At least not with one of Mark's maps,' Chris laughed.

As they walked up Town Road, Julie said, 'There's nobody in at my house today. Do you want to come back and eat with me?'

'That sounds fun. Can I phone the kiddies at yours?'

'Of course. Will we go to the Lion later?'

'Let's see what we feel like after eating. When do you think your kiddies get back?'

'They've gone to the beach with sis. They like to stop at a pub somewhere on the way back. They usually get in about ten.'

'I wonder if there's any films on the television? Could we watch something tonight?'

'If there's anything on. You can look in the Radio Times when we get back.'

Simon had to ask. 'Have you heard from Tim?'

'No. I wonder if he's still with Mary? Has Nick said anything to you about them?'

'I haven't seen him. None of us have. He's either been in Southleigh, or staying in to save money to get to Southleigh.'

Julie gently took Simon's hand in hers. Whether for reassurance, or to show she didn't care about Tim, or because she genuinely wanted to hold his hand, he wasn't sure.

They walked in silence, and then Julie said: 'Do you like chow mein?'

'I don't know. What is it?'

'Chinese. Noodles. Like spaghetti. And beef. Vegetables! A sauce. Have you never had Chinese food, choppy-socky kung fu boy?'

'No. My family are your average pork chop and cabbage kind of people. I think mum would call chow mein fancy foreign muck.'

'Well, I think there's a Vesta chow mein in the cupboard at home. We can try that.'

Simon rather liked the sound of it. 'I'll give it a go.' Julie was right. He did kung fu. He did tai chi. Eating Chinese food would make sense. The nearest he had so far come to Chinese food was chips and curry sauce from the take-away. He had also had a bite of a spring roll. James and Imogen were more adventurous, and had gone for meals in the Chinese Dragon. They had even drunk green tea. But they were the children of the middle class – well-off, bold, most enterprising, and well-informed. To eat Chinese food was expected of them.

Simon followed Julie through the gate, and up the garden

path to the house. The house was empty, as Julie had said it would be. They went along the hallway to the kitchen.

'Would you like a drink?' Julie said. 'Something cold?'

'A cup of tea would be nice.'

'I'll join you.' Julie's filled an electric kettle with water, and then switched it on. Julie's family was lower middle-class, but on the up. Either Julie or her sister would go to university, like Simon. And like Simon, Julie had another year before she need make any decisions. At least she too would be in town. Simon would still be able to see her, whatever choices she or he finally made. Even if she did return to Tim, or he and Anna did get together, it was good that she would still be around, that he could still say hello to her, would still be able to talk nonsense with her.

As if prompted by his unuttered thoughts, Julie put her arms around him and leaned into him. She looked up at him, and kissed him quickly. Simon liked these moments, but they also now confused him. The kettle switched itself off. They moved apart then, and Julie made tea for them.

'So, where's the *Radio Times*?' Simon said.

'Front-room,' Julie said. 'On the coffee table.'

He found the magazine, and opened it to the page for today as he walked back along the hallway. Julie was sitting at a round table, her blonde hair shining in the bright sun that came through a window in the large kitchen. Simon sat on a spindle-back chair beside her.

Julie sipped her tea. 'Anything?' she asked.

'A film with Alan Ladd. *This Gun for Hire*. Sounds interesting. But that's not until midnight. There is, of course, *Starsky and Hutch* before that.'

'I'm not a fan,' Julie said. 'It's the knitwear.'

'There's a play on BBC2 at nine.'

Julie shook her head, and then lit a cigarette.

Simon closed the magazine. 'No *TV Times*?'

'We only buy the *Radio Times*. We look in the paper for ITV. We don't watch it much, anyway. Only films.'

'Your mum doesn't like *Coronation Street?*'

Julie shook her head and blew a long plume of smoke from between her tightly pursed lips. Her eyes sparkled as smoke drifted and dust danced in the sunlight still falling through the window. 'She must be one of the few women in Britain who doesn't. She thinks soaps are silly. That's not real life, she says. Too dramatic.'

'It causes arguments at our house. Mum must watch *Coronation Street* every week. But Dad sometimes wants to watch a film on the other channel, or a documentary. He asks nicely. Mum says no. He then notes that mum watches it every single week. Mum says she won't know what's happening if she doesn't watch this week's episode. And so it goes. He tries, but he never wins.'

Julie crushed out her cigarette. 'He never will.'

'I know that. I think he knows that, as well.'

'So what will we do?'

'Go to The Lion?'

'I don't have much money.'

'Neither do I. Could you bear another perambulation around the leafy byways of Dereham?'

'If that means a walk with you, then always.'

Simon felt his heart flutter a little. Even though everything seemed to have changed since last weekend, still there were times when Julie looked at him and smiled with those shining eyes when he wanted this summer to stand still *here*, right at this instant, so that he could gather to his heart every bushel of it to shore against the grey that would surely come.

'Let's go to Derebury for a change,' Julie said.

'I don't know,' Simon said. 'That's a bit close to Copsehill, and we know there'll be madness over there tonight. We don't want to get ourselves mixed up with crazy people.'

'I'm sure it won't be that bad. Will it?'

135

'Hah! Paul is up from Devon, which means dubious occult practices. Of course, James is involved, which probably means acid, but almost certainly means brandy. And Charlie is there, which means heavy vibes.'

'Hmm. Well, when you put it like that, perhaps *Starsky and Hutch* wouldn't be so bad.'

'But then Derebury is a mile or so away from Copsehill, and they'll stay there. Particularly if they're off their heads.'

'All right. As long as you protect me from any demons they might conjure up.'

'You'll be safe with me.'

Julie looked at Simon, her blue eyes soft. 'Yes. I know. I would always be safe with you. I know that.' She came over to him and put her arms around him. Simon softly kissed the top of her head.

'We should make the chow mein,' Julie said.

'I'm looking forward to it,' Simon said. 'I have no idea how you cook it, though.'

'Cook is too strong a word for what we do,' Julie said. 'It's more like magic. And I am your magician.' She favoured Simon with a look of mystery and went to the cupboard.

'Have you made it before?' Simon said, raising an eyebrow as she returned with a box, studying the instructions.

'Well, no. But it looks simple enough. At least it does when my mum does it.'

She looked quickly at the back of the box one more time. Simon took the box from her. He read the instructions while Julie found pans in which she could heat the beef chow mein and fry the crispy noodles.

'Are you're sure you know how to do this?' Simon said.

Julie put the frying pan on a hob, and poured a little oil into it. She turned on the gas, and ignited it. 'It can't be that difficult. Fry the noodles, and then heat the chow mein. Easy-peasy.'

Julie put the dried chow mein into a saucepan, and then added some water to it. She lit the ring under the saucepan, and turned it down low to simmer. 'I just have to heat this through,' she said. She stirred the chow mein with a wooden spoon, and then turned back to the frying pan. 'Do you think the oil is hot enough yet?'

'How would I know? I don't even know what a noodle is.'

'True.' Julie looked closely at the pan.

'Did you ever make this for Tim?' Simon said.

'No. You will be the first person I've ever made this for. Actually, you might be the first boy I've ever cooked for.'

'Well, that's one in the eye for Tim,' Simon said. Although he knew Tim had tasted other delights, and Simon envied him that.

'Do you think the oil is hot enough now?'

'You keep asking me these questions as if I could possibly know the answers.'

'I'm not sure.'

'We could experiment.'

'You mean, throw one noodle in? Just like that?'

'Yes. Go on. Be brave.'

Julie took two noodles from the bag, and dropped them in the pan. They slowly curled and absorbed all the fat.

'I would suggest,' Julie said, 'that the fat isn't quite hot enough for noodles yet.'

Julie found a fork, removed the fatty noodles from the pan, and then added more oil.

Simon and Julie closely observed the oil. 'A watched pan never... uh-' Simon said. 'Well, what does oil do? Does it boil?'

'That's like poetry that is. I don't know. I suppose it must.' Julie stirred the chow mein.

They watched the frying pan for a few moments. It began to smoke. 'Go for it,' Simon said.

Julie took some of noodles from the bag and threw them into the pan. They began to curl. 'That's hot enough, I'm sure.' She tipped the whole bag into the pan.

'You're very sure of yourself,' Simon said.

'It's time.' Julie leaned across and kissed Simon. 'It was time for some of that, too.'

Simon watched the noodles curling and crisping, turning yellow and burning a little. 'How long now?'

'Try this one,' Julie said. She stabbed a noodle with a fork. 'Open wide.' She popped the noodle into Simon's mouth.

Simon frowned as he chewed. 'I'm not sure. It's like... plastic, like rubber, very fatty.' He managed to swallow it. 'That can't be right. Please let it not be right.'

Julie frowned in turn. 'No, that's not right.' She forked a noodle into her own mouth. She chewed cautiously, and then she nodded. 'Ah! Mine is good! You got one of the first ones.' She offered Simon another noodle. This noodle was much better, crispy, it crunched pleasingly between his teeth. 'Well, that's better. I must compliment you on your excellent culinary skills.'

Julie danced over to a cupboard. She picked out plates, and put them on the table. She grabbed forks for them both from the drainer. She tipped some noodles on to each plate, and ladled out the chow mein equally.

'Sit down, Simon,' Julie said. She turned off the burners on the cooker, and then put the pans into the bowl in the sink. 'You're about to experience foreign muck.'

She sat down next to him, and picked up her fork. 'Don't be afraid. Eat it all up.' She looked across at him then. Simon returned the look. The sun shone through the window. Her eyes, the eyes he had looked into so often this summer, were as blue as the bright sky and as warm as the sun. The irises were flecked with gold. He took a careful mouthful of the chow mein. It tasted good. Oily, beefy, spicy, sharp, piquant, crunchy. There were flavours here he'd never tasted before. More novelty in this summer of discovery.

'What do you think of chow mein?' Julie said.

'Brilliant,' Simon said. 'It's brilliant. Everything. This food. That sky. Your eyes. This summer. Your face. Every single thing.'

*

Some hours later, they were lying on their backs on an embankment at Derebury. They had followed various roads and paths out of town before climbing the steep slopes of the hill. From here, they had a view over the town towards the South Wiltshire downs, and Copse and Red Post hills.

The sun was setting at the honeyed horizon. *Every single thing.* Simon wondered what he had been feeling. Whatever it was, it had been intense. Thin cirrus striped the sun and flamed orange. The evening was still. He had felt something like it with Anna before the summer. This, though, had been, in that moment, more intense. He wasn't sure what was happening. Was it the blue skies, the summer heat, the blue eyes, the moment, the face, her smile? In the eastern quarter the sky was shading to violet-blue. Simon was certain he could see movement on the road at Copsehill – the Prophets getting up to mischief. He thought he saw somebody on the ridge path between Red Horn and Copsehill, and light from a torch, but he wasn't sure. He hoped it wasn't skywatchers; they would *not* find kindred souls on the hill tonight.

'Have you seen Sarah lately?' Simon said.

Julie lit a cigarette. 'Yes, we went to the pub during the week. It was fine.'

'You'd think Sarah would have a boyfriend.'

'You would.' Julie said uncertainly, and picked at some of the brittle, brown grass. 'Do you like Sarah? Would you go out with her?'

'Sarah is pleasantly... *pneumatic.*'

'Pneumatic?' Julie said. 'What does that mean?'

'It's from TS Eliot. *Uncorseted, her friendly bust/Gives promise of pneumatic bliss.*'

'Oh, I see. I think.'

'Huxley uses the word too, in that sense. He describes Lenina Crowne as pneumatic. In fact, *wonderfully* pneumatic.'

'So, are we talking about breasts?'

'Could be.'

'Fancy you remembering all those quotes.'

'Only because they mentioned breasts, of course. I only read Eliot for the smut.'

Julies laughed. 'So, are we saying ... I mean, are *you* saying, Sarah has large breasts?'

'Perhaps.'

'Well, haven't I?'

'To be honest,' Simon said, 'I've never really noticed. I mean, I've looked at them, don't get me wrong. I don't think you're boy or anything.'

'I am relieved.'

'Except when you're wearing *King Arthur's Avalon*.'

'Well, of course.'

'So, yes. I've never really thought about, uh, the size, of your, uh... you know. They are *not* the first thing I notice about you.'

'So what do you notice first?'

'Your eyes.'

'My eyes?'

'Yes. They are blue. Very blue. Like the sky this summer. And they sparkle.'

Julie smiled, but Simon couldn't quite tell now if the smile was one of shyness or of disbelief. 'But aren't they a little narrow?' she said. 'Don't you think I look like Clint Eastwood?'

'Yes, Clint with breasts. I just don't know their size.'

'Are you thinking of my eyes or my breasts?'

Simon laughed. 'Your eyes. Your eyes might be narrow, I don't know. I don't know what that means. What does that mean? Narrow compared to what? I mean, obviously you're not doe-eyed-'

'*Obviously.* Thanks for reminding me.'

'But... and there is a but... your eyes shine. They coruscate. I like to make you smile, because then the light dances in your eyes.'

'Really?' Julie said and light danced in her eyes.

Simon fell for a moment, a giddying moment in which the Earth lifted and spun. And just for that moment there was not enough breath left in the whole world. And then Julie punched him lightly on the arm.

'You great big enormous flirt,' she said. She brushed some strands of his long fair hair away from his face. 'I've always liked your eyes, too. A deep blue. And flirty, like you.'

They were silent for a few moments. Simon rolled over on his back. Long stalks of grass drooped over him. 'You know, we also call her the Coventry Climax.'

'Who? Sarah?'

'Yes.'

'Why?'

'Well, she works in the banana factory—'

'Sometimes it's like Innuendo City around here.'

'Yes. Indeed. Anyway, they have fork lift trucks. That's their name. The make and the model. Pneumatic Sarah, the Coventry Climax.'

'I see. I hope *you* would never call her that.'

Simon shook his head. 'Why, of course not. When I say we, I mean Nick, Mark and Gaz. It was Nick, of course, who came up with that name.'

'Ah yes, Nick. A cad and a bounder.'

'He is. I shake my head and tut loudly whenever he uses that name for her.'

Simon rolled over onto his side. He wanted to see Julie's eyes again. Julie was already on her side, her cheek resting against her hand. She looked at him, smiling gently, warmly. The world again tilted slightly, but then Julie looked at her watch, and that action was so mundane it set the globe aright.

'We should continue our walk,' Julie said.

Simon sighed. 'If we must.' He looked at the embankment to his right. It circled the top of Derebury, and provided an easy, level path around the hill.

Julie leaned over and kissed him lightly. 'We can go around

the top and then back into town, to the Lion. We can put our money together and get us both a drink.'

Simon's world steadied. Something about the air up here was dizzying, something about the light was disorienting, something in the moment needed a question, and an answer. *Something.* But he *was* still Simon, despite everything that had happened this summer. And there was time yet for a hundred indecisions and a hundred visions and revisions.

They climbed to the top of the embankment and followed it as darkness deepened. Many footsteps over many years had worn a path through the grass and topsoil to the grey flint and white chalk beneath. The path showed faintly before them, a thin pale strand in the night. As they walked, Simon and Julie talked of Imogen and James, Stuart and Kate, and Nick and Heather. They wondered what state of inebriation the Prophets had reached, what drugs they had taken. Simon thought James had certainly dropped a tab.

'Imogen will be so annoyed,' Julie said. 'I wonder if they've conjured a demon yet.'

They walked slowly along the path. They were on the north of Derebury now, and the hill fell away from them to the Plain. They stopped sometimes and embraced each other. Sometimes, they tentatively kissed each other. Simon was unsure now when to kiss Julie. A week ago, everything had been simple. But since then, his shyness had been returning. Was it shyness or fear, Simon wondered. And Julie had been withdrawing from him. Nonetheless, when he and Julie embraced, the world turned giddily but pleasantly, and things happened in his stomach and chest. None of it felt bad. Julie still favoured him with short kisses; kisses that were even softer than last week and yet still gave him sweet, innocent pleasure. Better this than nothing. After all, the future might hold only nothing.

Julie turned and skipped away from Simon. She was wearing a dark tee shirt, and jeans. As she moved further along the path, only her bare arms and blonde hair were visible. Simon wondered what the time was, and whether they would make it to the Lion tonight. He thought it unlikely. Not that he cared. Nick was probably out with Heather somewhere, so only Mark and Gaz would be in the pub. Mark would be watching Chrissie and Jake, while Gaz would be, as usual, rude and abrupt. Simon would much rather be out here with on this warm hill with Julie, following the pale chalk thread that led them onward, with the happy dancing girl ahead of him.

Simon wished he could scry the dancing girl's thoughts. He held back from asking what they might be, because that would inevitably lead to the Anna problem, and that would only lead to serious talk. He enjoyed the playfulness too much to allow that. He and Julie weren't *together*, after all, so there was no need to become *serious*. And yet, perhaps they *were* together in some romantic way he couldn't fathom. No-one else thought of them as a couple – well, not so far as he knew, anyway. Perhaps his friends did think of them that way. Were they *going out*? Well, they were out. They still sometimes kissed. Their intimacies hadn't progressed very far beyond that. He wasn't sure how they would progress beyond that, and was even less certain that Julie wanted such progression. Simon knew he knew nothing of these things. He was, however, certain about one thing – there was nothing he'd rather be doing this still, warm night than walking around this chalk-necklaced hilltop with Julie skipping ahead of him, and stopping sometimes to watch stars blink through the heat-hazed sky.

Simon called to Julie. 'Hey, Jules, what's the time?'

Julie stopped walking. 'Eleven-thirty!' There was surprise in her voice. 'How did that happen?'

'Well, we've saved a quid or two.'

'Yes. I can get buy some fags tomorrow, now.' As if reminded of her addiction, Julie found a cigarette and lit it. The lighter flame flared brightly in the darkness.

Simon and Julie walked on. They were now on the eastern side of Derebury Hill. Here, the hill gently fell away to The

Tump, and Red Post Farm, and to the road to Copsehill. Julie sat on the edge of the embankment overlooking the ditch fifteen feet beneath her. Simon sat with her.

'We're not in a rush, are we?' Julie said.

'No,' Simon said. 'I am thirsty, though. We should have thought to bring a drink with us.'

'Would you like to come to my house when we get back into town? For a coffee, or tea?'

'Oh, yes,' Simon said. She must know he would. 'Of course. That'll be great.'

Julie leaned her head on Simon's shoulder. Now, they could see the town lights of Dereham beneath them, orange and yellow street lamps. Simon could hear shouts, voices, and the sounds of radios, televisions, and car engines drifting up the hill on the still air. The pubs were emptying. By the time he and Julie arrived in town, the streets would be clear. There was a film on television tonight, Simon thought. He reminded Julie.

'What was it?'

'Some gangster movie, I think.

'Who was in it? You told me.'

'Alan Ladd.'

'When does it start?'

'Some time around midnight.

'Would you like to sit and watch it with me?'

'Well, yes. As long as your kiddies don't mind.'

If we keep quiet, they'll be fine. I just hope sis isn't watching anything.'

'I'd be happy with a cuppa and more chat.'

Julie kissed him on the cheek then. 'You're lovely, you know that?' She stood.

'When you tell me, I have to believe it.'

'Come on, hippie boy. Let's go see Alan Ladd and get a cuppa.'

'Is he running a joint in town?' Simon said.

'I wouldn't go there even if he did. It's probably full of gangsters and cowboys.'

Julie pulled Simon up. She dusted her jeans, and then, laughing, dusted down Simon's chinos. As she brushed dry grass and dust from the back of his legs and his bottom, Simon looked over towards Copsehill. He thought he saw light, a bright light that had only been there for a brief moment. He had no idea what it might have been.

'I've just seen a UFO,' Simon said.

Julie stopped patting him then, and stood up straight. She followed his gaze over Copsehill. 'You're joking.'

'No, there *was* a light over the hill. It was bright, but it just sort of... vanished.'

'What do you think it was?'

'I don't know. But one thing I'm sure of... It wasn't a flying saucer.'

'You big sceptic. What *do* you think it was?'

'The tail of a meteor, possibly'

'Come on,' Julie said. 'Let's go and watch some telly and drink tea.'

They followed the path around the embankment until they reached the southern entrance of the hillfort. Here the trackway into the fort was the footpath that led back to town. Everything from now on was downhill, for which Simon was grateful. He and Julie had already walked over ten miles today. Their progress was slow. The path was narrow, and they stopped sometimes to look at something – a satellite wandering across the sky, a constellation, the play of the light from the town on the branches of a tree. Sometimes they stopped to work out where they were going on a path that looked slightly different in the dark.

Simon felt a chill run down his spine. Julie suddenly stopped walking. Her hand was in Simon's, and she pulled him back to her. 'Simon, look, down there,' she whispered, and pointed.

He looked, but could see nothing. 'What?' he whispered.

'There's somebody, something, down there, in the trees.'

They were above another path that snaked through shrubs

and trees below them. Simon peered into the trees, but could see nothing there. Julie moved closer, and put an arm around his waist. She pulled him tight to her. Simon sensed her uneasiness and placed a reassuring arm around her.

'That was... freaky,' Julie said quietly.

'What was it?' Simon said. 'What did you see?'

'There was somebody down there, I'm sure there was. And I got the shivers.'

Simon said nothing. He wanted some light. 'Come on,' he said. 'Let's get into town before we're eaten by demons or ghouls or something like that.' He looked around him. He knew where he was now. They had to get onto the path where Julie had seen... whatever it was. They had little option; they would otherwise need to follow their current path around the bottom of the hill for another mile. 'Which way did the... person... ghost... uh, beast... go?'

Julie stopped for a moment, and pointed west. 'That way. Like ... it... was heading for the station.'

'Okay. So let's go the other way.'

'You're so brave,' Julie said. 'My hero.'

'I want to get back to yours unmolested. I need a cup of tea, not a mystery.'

They walked quickly and quietly along the path, and crossed a bridge over the railway line. They were soon under street lights, and slowed their walk.

'That's better, isn't it?' Simon said.

Julie nodded. 'I need a cigarette.' She lit one as they walked. 'Now don't laugh. And don't try to come up with rational explanations, you big handsome sceptic.'

'I won't. So, what manner of beast did you see?'

'I swear I saw a figure in a hat, a three-cornered hat, walking along the path. The figure became fainter and fainter and then disappeared.'

'But it's dark down there.'

'I know. But I really did see something strange. And I felt really cold,' Julie added.

'Yes. I got a shiver down my spine, too.'

'Really?' Julie said. 'You felt something?'

'I felt *something*, certainly,' Simon said. 'It might have been the same thing as you felt.'

'Of course it was the same thing. It was a *ghost*. From days of yore. When they wore three-cornered hats.'

Simon didn't believe in ghosts, but he couldn't deny the sudden shiver. 'I have no idea what you saw,' he said. 'My mind is open to all ideas.' He pulled Julie to him, to reassure her. They walked beneath sodium-orange street lamps, still talking about what she had seen, and then drifted off onto other local ghost stories, Laughing Jack at Sleet Copse, the ghost on the washing line at Southleigh, the demon that pressed its face against the window of an old cottage in Barton Road.

By the time they arrived back at Julie's they were grateful for the banality of electric lights and the radio. Julie's father was in the kitchen, and greeted them both cheerily. Julie told him they were going to watch the end of the film, if that was all right. Mr Lawrence said of course it was, but asked them to keep the noise down as everybody else was in bed, and he was headed there himself.

Julie made tea for her and Simon. They went to the front room. Julie turned on the television and switched to BBC2. She pulled Simon onto the sofa with her. She put his arm around her shoulder and they relaxed together into the film. They hardly spoke as they drank their tea and watched Alan Ladd and Veronica Lake. They snuggled together on the sofa, and enjoyed each other's comfortable company after their day of exertion.

When the film finished, Simon was very tired. He had to go to his bed.

'We'll meet up again soon, yeah?' Julie said.

'Oh yes. I'm sure we will,' Simon replied.

He stood, and then offered Julie his hand. She took it, and he pulled her up. They embraced for the last time this evening. It had been another excellent summer's day.

147

Julie slipped her arm through Simon's as they walked along the hall to the front door. 'Do I have a name?'

'A name?'

'Yes, a nick-name.'

'Oh, yes,' Simon said. 'Miss Lovely. But that's my name for you, not a Nick nick-name.'

She kissed his cheek. 'Thank you for a splendid day.'

'Any time, Miss Lovely.'

Julie smiled. And for Simon, the world tilted again.

9

These Are Your Hopes and Fears

Julie stretched as she waited for Sarah. They would meet Simon, Mark, Nick and the others at Copsehill, where they would join the search for James. For James had gone missing during the skywatch the previous Saturday. No-one knew why, and nobody knew where he might be. Imogen was beside herself with worry, as were his parents, particularly his mother. His closest friends, Charlie, Stuart, and Paul, were bemused and confounded. Of course, James had dropped a tab that night as Simon had predicted he would. He could be dead in a ditch, he could be in a hospital. The police wanted to be sure that James wasn't somewhere in the area, so had brought in some local PCs to search. His friends had been asked to help, as they would know his favourite haunts.

Julie looked forward to seeing Simon. She had seen him only once during the past week. They'd had a chat and a drink in the Lion. People had come and gone while they were there, asking about James. Charlie had joined them at one point, worried about his friend, but at the same time talking excitedly about the UFO he had seen, and how he now thought aliens and flying saucers might be real. Charlie had always been a bit... *odd*... more on-edge than his laid-back friends – but now he appeared a tad manic, and wanted to talk to everybody, wanted to convince his friends that he had indeed experienced something unusual.

Julie couldn't talk to Simon about what she really wanted to talk about – which was *them*. Romance. A couple. She really enjoyed being with Simon. She'd finally sorted out her feelings about Tim. What she needed to know now was how Simon felt about Anna. And she remained uncertain about how Simon felt about *her*. He kissed her and hugged her. He was lovely. He drew her out. He helped her talk. She felt absorbed by him, and that he was absorbed by her. Yet there remained a barrier, a thin film she couldn't penetrate. Over the days since the party, they had kissed and embraced less often. Still, she wanted to be with him. She thought he wanted to be with her. She also felt that, for Simon, the kissing, the hugging, and whatever else might occur between them was peripheral. What seemed most important to him was simply being with her. This had its own charms. There was no pressure. There was no need to perform. She could be entirely herself. And, yes, during these summer days with Simon, she had realised his kind of life was what she wanted – long walks, conversation, books, and old films starring Alan Ladd. She needed to talk to Simon about this, and about her feelings. But her faltering attempts to do so that night had been constantly interrupted. That was, of course, under-standable. Because James had gone missing.

She'd never learned what Simon wanted, not that night at the pub. But she knew she was *Miss Lovely*. She knew he thought *everything* was brilliant. She remembered what he had said. The sky, her eyes, this summer, her face. *Everything.* She remembered it word for word, because that was how she felt, too.

On Wednesday, she'd bumped into Nick as he and Heather alighted from the Southleigh bus. They said they were going to the pub, and asked if she would like to join them. She said yes, because she needed to talk to one of Simon's friends. Nick had also wanted to talk to her, it turned out. Because he knew she'd been seeing a lot of Simon, and wanted to make sure everything was fine, that she wouldn't hurt him.

'He's kind of innocent,' Nick said.

'He's so nice to me,' Julie said. 'I feel comfortable with him.'

Nick laughed. 'If I had a penny for every girl who'd ever said *that* about the lovely Simon. You have no idea how jealous of him his friends have been.' He turned to Heather. 'You've met him, what, twice? What do you think of Si?'

'Lovely,' Heather said. 'That night at Mark's party, he couldn't have been more helpful. And when I talked to him while you were downstairs, he was most charming and very amusing.'

'So, what you're saying,' Julie said, 'is that I'm not so special. He charms everybody.'

'I don't think we are,' Heather said. 'I think we're saying you're lucky.'

'He likes you,' Nick added. 'I'm sure of that. I haven't seen him like this since before the summer, and Anna.'

'Ah, yes,' Julie said. 'Anna.' She had managed to forget about Anna. She was sure now of her feelings about Tim, but she had no idea how Simon felt about Anna. He had said little about her recently. She looked at Nick, then at Heather. 'Do either of you know Anna?'

Nick shook his head. 'Not really,' he said. 'I met her once at a noisy gig. Hardly said a word to her. They obviously liked each other. But that was six weeks ago. A lot of things have happened this summer, and you're one of them.'

Julie sighed, and leaned backwards in her chair. She lit a cigarette. She looked out of the window at the bright day. It had thundered on Sunday, all morning. Close, and very loud. Imogen had worried about James, lost in the hills in the pouring rain, tripping, getting hypothermia, having nightmares. But now those storms might never have happened. The summer they'd all known for so long had quickly reasserted itself, and the sun shone as bright ever. For two days the world had become green again, but now the grasses and leaves were returning to brown.

'You know Simon has never had a girlfriend *at all*, right?' Nick said.

Julie leaned forward again, and blew smoke towards the ceiling. 'Well, I kind of know that. I mean, we haven't talked about it. I know he's shy. He's unsure of himself.'

He's also afraid of rejection. And he feels he's unattractive. Because if he was attractive, girls would go out with him, right?'

'Well, only if he asks.'

'Right. But he's too shy to ask. And afraid. Afraid of the thing he hasn't done, afraid of rejection. And because he hasn't yet had a girlfriend, he feels unattractive. He's trapped in a vicious circle.'

'But haven't you talked to him?'

'Of course,' Nick said. 'But that first step is hard. I remember it well. He can't seem to manage it.'

'Probably psychological,' Heather said. 'He has a complex, or some unconscious desire or block.'

Nick grimaced. 'Heather is your basic Freudian nightmare.'

Heather kissed Nick. 'I'm better looking than old Sigmund, though,' she said.

Better looking than *me*, Julie thought. Better looking than most people. *Perhaps I'm not good enough for Simon. Not when there are Heathers in the world, and Imogens.* Perhaps that's what Simon really wanted. Perhaps that's what Anna was.

'Is Anna pretty?' Julie said, hating herself for asking.

Nick shrugged. 'I suppose. Not my type.'

'Long, lovely hair, right? Hippie girl?'

'Now, Jules, stop right there. Don't compare yourself to somebody else. Anything I say will make you feel bad. I've seen you and Si this summer. You've both had fun, you look happy. Ultimately, that's all that counts.'

And that was easy for Nick to say, she thought, because he had Heather leaning into him with her blonde hair and long legs and full breasts. Heather had many advantages. Too many other girls did. Julie needed to know that she and Anna were on a level playing field. She didn't know enough about Anna, and that distressed her. She might have to talk to Mark. Talking to Gaz would be useless.

Julie sucked on her cigarette, confused, and a little frustrated. 'Can't you point Si in the right direction?' she said to Nick.

'I will, of course. I already have. He doesn't believe me. He doesn't believe somebody as lovely as you might like him in that way.'

'He talks to you? About me?' Julie felt better knowing that.

'Yes. He talks to me about you. And he talks to Mark, and to Gaz.'

'Gaz?'

'Sadly, yes. Of course, he gets no sense out of Gaz, but they're old friends. Simon talks, Gaz ignores him. At least Simon lets it all out.' Nick twirled his glass between his fingers and looked at Julie cautiously. 'And Tim? You're no longer interested?'

Julie shook her head. 'No. No, I'm not.'

'You should just be Simon's best friend,' Nick said. 'And see how it goes.'

Heather nodded in agreement. 'Give him time. Let him come to you. It happened at the party, right?'

'I might be biased, because I'm one of his best friends,' Nick added. 'But I think it'll be worth the wait. It would be worth it for both of you.'

153

Julie had thanked them then, and left the pub feeling lighter than she had since the storms on Sunday morning. She wouldn't talk to Mark, or Gaz. She would see Simon, and let things slowly happen, if they did. And she would kiss him if she felt she should. And she would stop worrying.

During the week Julie watched films on the television, read magazines and paperback books and, all the time, looked forward to Saturday, when she would see Simon. Then Simon had phoned about the search. They agreed to meet at Copsehill. When Sarah heard about the search, she too wanted to join in. Sarah wasn't as close to the Prophets as Julie had been over the years, but she had been at school with James since primary school, and then through sixth-form.

The doorbell rang. 'That'll be Sarah,' Julie said to her mother, who sat at the kitchen table, reading the local newspaper. Her parents had also been shocked by James's disappearance. His parents lived a few hundred yards along the road from her house.

She put her knapsack over her shoulder. It promised to be another hot day, and her mother insisted she take plenty of drink with her.

Julie went to the front door. Sarah was waiting for her. They linked arms and walked down the drive and then out into Town Road. They headed towards the Market Place. At first, they only talked about James, and his disappearance. Then Sarah said, 'Tim isn't seeing Mary.'

'I know. Heather told me.'

'I saw him at The Swan last night.'

Julie shrugged 'So? I'm happy now.'

Sarah smiled knowingly. 'With Simon.'

Sarah offered Julie a cigarette. Julie took one.

'Yes, with Simon.' Julie had seen Sarah during the week, and they had talked about Simon and Tim. 'But as I told you, we're not an item. We just enjoy each other's company. It might seem strange, a long courtship in this day and age, but I like it. It's relaxing. If nothing comes of it, I don't care.'

'So you said.'

'I know. But it's worth repeating. I missed him and his friends, the Prophets, Honeyhouse. I liked that world. I liked them.

'Won't you miss nightclubs? Or the chance of going to the races, or to a fancy restaurant, or... I don't know, a Grand Prix?'

'I used to think that. But then I realised that's kind of nonsense. Mark and Gray like bikes and cars. James and Imo go to Bath races. Simon and Nick go to clubs sometimes. Charlie and Gaz go to Ashton Gate to watch the football. Okay, so they do all those things less often than Tim and his friends. But Si and his friends do other things. They talk. There's the band. The walks. They read. I don't think Tim has read a book since school except Sven Hassel.'

'Are you sure *I'm* good enough for you?' Sarah said, and then smiled cheekily.

Julie pulled Sarah close to her reassuringly. 'Of course, you are you big silly. I'm not saying Tim's bad because he doesn't read. I'm just saying I like to read.'

'So we can still be seen together?

Julie laughed. 'Of course we can, you big 'nana.'

They walked into the Market Place.

'Soooo,' Sarah said. 'You and Simon are not an item.'

'Not yet.'

'Do you think you ever will be?'

'Perhaps. I'm enjoying what there is. It's been a dazzling summer.'

'Oh, I don't know,' Sarah said. 'The heat gets a bit wearing after a while.'

'But the colours, Sarah! The blues, the golds, the sunset orange and yellow-'

Sarah bumped Julie with her shoulder. 'Some of us are not in love.'

'I'm not in love,' Julie said. And then she heard the words to the song in her head. 'And don't forget it.'

They were on the narrow path that led out of the Market Place into the car park behind the post office. There were few cars here this morning.

'Mary knows Anna,' Sarah said. She said it blithely, as if she hadn't considered the impact of saying it.

Julie felt her stomach knot. 'Really?'

'Mary told Tim everything. He told me the other night.' Sarah turned and looked at her friend. 'You must have wondered about her.'

They reached New Road and turned west. The sun was suddenly hot. Julie wished she still had the trilby. 'Yes. Of course. Go on. What she's like.'

'*Funny.*'

'What else?'

'You sure you want to hear this?'

Sarah might be Julie's best friend, but Julie knew how it worked. Sarah had gossip, and it was a hot potato, burning her palm. She had to pass it on. Gossip had a life of its own. Julie *wanted* to hear it, even though it might be painful; that was the awful thing.

Julie nodded. 'Go on. Tell me.'

Sarah told Julie what she knew. 'And she's good looking,' Sarah finished. 'At least, that's what Mary told Tim.'

Julie felt the tension in her stomach again. Of course, Anna would be pretty. She'd be an Imo, or a Heather. Not a Julie.

'Anna really likes Simon,' Sarah continued. '*Really* likes him. She can't wait to get back to college.'

'Oh,' said Julie. To her own ears, it sounded like a cross between an O! of surprise and an Ow! 'He's a lovely boy,' she said. 'I'm not surprised by that. But it's why we're not together in that way,' she added, aware that she was improvising a story about herself on the spot, and wondering why she would do this with Sarah. 'The Anna thing. And there was Tim. And that made everything tricky. But I'm free of Tim now, and–'

'Are you really, though?' Sarah said. 'Because, you know, if Si is waiting for Anna, then why wait for him?'

'I'm not waiting for him. And Tim is not for me.'

'He says he misses you.'

'Yeah, right. He misses sex. He shouldn't have been such a... pig. And so boring. But he *was*. And the problem for Tim is that now I'm out here in this beautiful, sun-filled world, I like it here. Simon or not.'

'Hanging around with Simon has made you all poetical.'

Julie blushed, and this time she bumped Sarah with her shoulder. Sarah bumped in return. They walked in silence for a while, past the encopsed Tump on their right, through the tunnel of trees with their shrivelled brown leaves, and then on past Red Post Farm. Now Julie could see other people on the road ahead of them, walking slowly up the next slope, heading towards Copsehill. It looked like Jake and Chrissie. Julie was surprised they were here. But, then, Mark would have mentioned the search to them, and everyone liked James. She hoped Tim wouldn't be here. She doubted he would be. These weren't his people. Julie was grateful that Sarah now talked about music, about Pilot, 10cc, Rod Stewart and Fleetwood Mac.

When Julie and Sarah finally arrived at the gates that blocked the roads beneath the summit of Copsehill, they found a large group of their friends mingling with policemen of various ranks. Normally, the proximity of so many policemen would be cause for concern for the likes of Danny and John, but everyone appeared relaxed. The policemen were in uniform, but their helmets were off, their ties were loose, and their coats unbuttoned. Julie looked around. Tim wasn't here. Simon sat on the grass bank with Mark, Chrissie, and Jake. Simon gave her a wave. Imogen was with Kate and Stuart. They stood with a policeman who was obviously in charge of today's operation. Imogen's face was drawn, troubled. There were dark rings under her eyes. Her long curly hair was tangled. Julie couldn't see Charlie.

She was standing next to Steve, from the band. 'Where's Charlie?' she asked him.

'Ah, yes. Charlie,' Steve said. 'He's in Devon. He'd already arranged to go there and see Jane. You know about them?' Julie nodded. 'He wanted to help, but he'd already bought a ticket for the train.'

'Who's the guy with Imo?'

'A senior police officer,' Steve said. 'A detective or something.'

At that moment, the detective-or-something clapped his hands to get everybody's attention. He introduced himself, and explained what they were going to do today. The police would search the fields around the area where James had last been seen. His friends were to organise themselves into small groups and begin fanning out over the fields, looking for anything that might lead to James.

When the detective finished talking, Sarah said: 'You want to be with Si, don't you?'

Julie shrugged, but Sarah was right.

'You go on over,' Sarah said. 'You probably need to talk to him. I'll go with Steve and Danny.'

'Thanks, Sarah.' Julie went to Simon. Mark, Chrissie and Jake still sat with him. They were quite at ease in each other's company, despite the fight at Mark's party two weeks ago. She said hello to them. She wanted to ask if they had all kissed and made up, but thought it best not to mention anything in case this congeniality was in fact a fragile charade.

Simon looked up at her. 'Hello, there.' He reached up and wrapped two fingers around the fingers of her left hand. 'How are you, Jules?'

She crouched down beside him and knitted the rest of her fingers through his. 'I'm good.' She wondered if she would tell him any of what Sarah had told her. She wanted this walk, this search, to be uneventful, for her sake, for Imogen's sake. She couldn't face telling Simon that Anna was waiting for him.

'I'll be back in a mo,' she said. Everyone was getting ready to move. People examined maps and talked to each other, planning where they would go, and with whom. The policemen were already walking into the field where James and Paul had held their silly ritual.

Julie went to Imogen and embraced her. 'I'm sorry about James,' Julie said. She stood apart from her then and looked in Imo's sad brown eyes. 'We'll find something today, I'm sure.'

'I do hope so,' Imogen said. 'Thank you for coming and helping with this. I appreciate it.'

'Where should we go?'

Stuart was holding a map. He pointed at it as he gave her instructions. When he finished, he said: 'Just tell Simon what I told you. He'll know the way.'

Julie nodded. 'I'll tell him. We'll see you back here later.' She turned and signalled to Simon. He and the others stood then, and brushed the dust and grass from themselves. Julie told Simon what Stuart had said. Chrissie, Jake and Mark also listened. They knew roughly where the paths led. Mark and Simon were pleasantly surprised that they were allowed to walk along the old Lavington Road further than they ever had before without fear of Range Control or the police turning them back. They climbed over the gate. The road was crumbling, and there were potholes everywhere. Jake and Chrissie walked at the rear of the group, talking together, scanning the long, shining, dry white grass of the Plain. Julie walked between Simon and Mark. They scanned the short grass and flinty chalk of the track. The sun was high now, and the rest of the afternoon would be hot.

Julie looked at Simon, and smiled. 'I wish I still had the trilby.'

'Oh, yes,' Simon said. 'The trilby. You did look very sweet in that. I should have brought it with me. I wasn't sure that you'd be here.'

'It's James,' she said. 'Of course, I'd be here. A lot of people are here for him.'

Simon took her hand again, then. They walked slowly, looking around them. Julie had become comfortable with Simon's hand over the summer. It felt right. She worried now, though, about

Simon and Anna. What Sarah had said preyed on her mind. She knew she should tell Simon what Sarah had told her, but she couldn't. She couldn't tell him. Not *now*. As they walked, they all talked of serious things – what could have happened to James, where he might be or might have gone – and then inconsequential things – music, and motorbikes, and cricket, and the glorious weather, and the thunderstorms last weekend. Weaving through it all was Julie's refusal to say anything about Anna to Simon. They were heading up Hawthorn Lane now, an hour into the walk, and she had said still nothing. She knew now that she wouldn't. Even though Simon had become such a close friend over the summer, she couldn't tell him. Even worse, she had realised over the course of their long walk that if Mary knew Anna, Simon could now get Anna's address, and he wouldn't even need to wait for the start of term, a month away, to meet up with Anna again.

Julie knew now how much she liked Simon. Because she couldn't bear to hear him talk about *his* Anna. She wasn't cruel and heartless. She didn't want Simon all to herself. She knew that Simon and Anna would meet at the start of the term, and then what would be, would be. *Que sera, sera*, as Doris sang. No, she wouldn't tell him because she couldn't bear to hear him thank her, and then say how happy he was to find out about Anna at last, how great it would be to see her, and perhaps – treating Julie like a friend – tell her how very lovely Anna was, how very gorgeous. It had been bad enough hearing it from Sarah. To hear it now from Simon's own lips would be too much. She had enjoyed this shining summer with Simon far too much to let her own honesty cloud the sun.

Que sera, sera. She had made peace with herself about Tim and now she would let Simon's own heart guide him.

A couple of hours later, Simon, Mark and Julie sat on the grassy bank at Copsehill. Chrissie and Jake had returned home. Other groups of friends had straggled in, and then either stayed on for news from Imogen or the police, or had wandered back into town. The afternoon heat had been relentless, and people were understandably tired. Julie and Mark were smoking, and swigging from drinks bottles they had brought with them. Julie shared her warm drink with Simon.

Finally, Imogen returned. She talked to the policeman in charge, while Kate and Stuart joined Simon, Mark and Julie.

'Did you find anything?' Simon said.

'Not a thing,' Stuart said.

'Same here.'

Imogen came over then, as the policemen began to drift away, walking into Dereham or climbing into vans and cars and driving back to their various hometowns. She was frowning. 'There was nothing,' she said. 'Nobody found anything. Not the police, and not our friends.' Her mouth set into a tight line. She spoke angrily. 'Where is the stupid little hippie?' Kate put an arm around her. Imogen rubbed tiredness from her face with dusty palms. 'Who's up for doing it again?' she said. 'Let's give it another go.'

'Where would we search now?' Danny said.

Imogen shook her head. There was tiredness and frustration in her voice. 'Oh, I don't know. Stuart? Kate?'

Stuart leaned over, and stroked her arm. 'We'll do the big circuit, over to Derebury and back. It's about five miles in total.' He looked around the others. 'If you're tired, drop out, don't worry.'

They all stood again. Julie needed time alone with her thoughts. She kissed Simon on the cheek, and said she'd see him down the Lion. Imogen came over, put an arm around Julie and thanked her. Then Julie walked down the road from Copsehill, towards Red Post Farm and Dereham, while the others climbed a stile and headed towards Derebury.

Julie needed a shower, and something to eat, but as she walked through town she saw Nick and Heather enter the Lion. She could afford a lemonade and needed to know what Heather knew. She slowed her pace. She couldn't afford to enter into buying rounds; best let Nick get Heather's drink first.

When Julie finally entered the bar, Nick and Heather were already seated. She waved and bought a drink, and then went over to their table. 'Do you mind if I join you for a while?' She said. 'I'm just going to drink this, and then I'm heading on home.'

'Of course not,' Nick said. 'No Simon?'

'He's still out on the hills. Stuart suggested one more circuit for those who could manage it. I couldn't.'

'Ah, yes, the search. Did anybody find anything?'

Julie shook her head. 'No. Nothing. Nor did the police.' She took a cigarette from her packet, and then offered the pack to Heather. She was grateful that Heather didn't take one. She only had these ten for the night. She lit her cigarette, and then wondered how to begin talking to Heather about Mary and Tim.

'I saw Mary today,' Heather said, initiating precisely the conversation Julie desired. 'She's not with Tim.'

Julie nodded. 'Yes, I know that. Sarah told me. She also told me something else. She said that Tim said that Mary knew Anna, the girl Simon likes.'

Tim laughed. 'Who said what said what?'

'Anna?' Heather said. 'Anna who?'

'I don't know. I don't think Simon knows either. The thing is, Sarah said Tim said Mary said-' Julie paused. 'It's like Chinese whispers, isn't it?'

'Pretty much,' Nick said.

'So. Mary knows Anna's sister.'

Heather raised a well-defined eyebrow. 'I know pretty much everybody that Mary knows. I've never heard of an Anna. Anne, yes. Annie. But not Anna. Where does she live?'

'In one of the villages near Southleigh. But Simon's not sure which.'

'I'm sure Mary knows no Annas, nor has friends with sisters called Anna,' Heather said. 'And certainly not in the villages. We only know a few girls from out there. So what did Mary say?'

Julie repeated what Sarah had told her.

Heather frowned and lit her own cigarette, a king-size Benson and Hedges that Julie envied. 'Mary hasn't seen Tim for a few days. Do you know what I think? Tim made this up. He's trying to make you jealous.'

'Do you think so?'

'Yes, I do.'

Nick looked at Julie. 'Did it work?'

'Kind of. But I did realise something.'

'What?' Nick said.

'I really like Simon. But I'm not sure how he feels about me.'

'We talked about this the other day. He's shy. Confused.'

'Yes, I know. And I know he likes me. But how much?'

'Quite a lot, I think,' said Heather. 'I hardly know him, but I see it.'

'But what if it's not quite enough? And what if I do say something, and Simon just gives me that smile, that lovely smile, and says yes, *but*.'

Nick shrugged and frowned. 'You could wait for Simon to say something first.'

'That might be a long wait.' Julie swigged down the remainder of her drink and stubbed out her cigarette. 'Anyway, I'll leave you two to canoodle. Will you be here later?'

'Yeah, sure,' Heather said. 'See you then.'

'Thanks for the help,' Julie said.

Julie walked back out into the sultry heat of the evening. The sun was lowering now, and the sky between the chimney pots was yellow, orange and red. She walked home a little lighter, yet still troubled by how confusing this had all become. She hadn't expected to feel any of this. And yet it had all been worth it, the sunshine, and the walks, and being with Simon, however

163

slightly out of kilter she now felt. After all, the whole hot summer had been completely out of kilter.

Later that evening, Julie met Simon at the White Lion. The pub was bustling, although there was no sign of Imogen and Kate. Imogen had gone to Kate's house, Stuart said, and he would be going there later. Julie sat next to Simon, but she resisted holding his hand, or kissing him, or putting her arm around him. Simon still looked at her in the same way, touched her arm when he talked, embraced her with his being, but no longer hugged her to him, no longer moved to kiss her lips. She missed him. He knew that something was happening, but wasn't sure what. Poor, shy Simon. He would be as baffled as ever at the end of all this, still not sure what to do with girls, still not sure whether one had liked him this summer, or had ever liked him. She wanted to tell him how she felt, but the fear of that smiling face saying that he wanted to be with Anna, not her, continued to stay her words.

The conversations in the pub revolved around James, and Imogen, and the craziness that had led to James going missing.

'It makes you think, doesn't it?' Mark said.

'What does it make us think?' Julie said.

'That it could be any of us. We don't know what's going to happen, even though we're all still young. Do you remember Duncan Smith? Died in an accident at work. Sixteen years old. And a part-time job! And now James has disappeared. Might be dead for all we know.'

Julie shook her head. 'Don't say that.'

Mark shrugged. 'Makes you think. Perhaps I should go for it with Chrissie. Or give up all hope of Chrissie. Perhaps it's time I made a decision one way or the other.'

'Yes, perhaps you should,' Julie said. Mark was right, of course. It did make you think. Perhaps she *should* speak to Simon. Except in her head remained that voice, Simon's voice, saying he liked Anna.

Still, she spent a pleasant evening in the pub with her old friends, and with Simon. He was still close to her. He wanted to touch her, to kiss her, to hug her, she knew it. And she still wanted him to. When time was called Mark suggested they all come back to his house. There was a discussion about who was going where. Jake and Chrissie were going back to Jake's place. Nick and Heather wanted a walk. Gray had his mother's car, and had to get the Mini back on the drive before midnight. Those leaving said their farewells.

At the house, Mark found drinks for them all. The conversation was drifting, as it often did in Dereham, around flying saucers, and music, and telepathy and ghosts. Mark said he'd do a tarot reading for everyone. Chris thought it a splendid idea.

Simon shook his head. 'Not for me.'

'Go on, Julie,' Mark said. 'You must have your cards read. Let's see what fate awaits you.'

'Oh, all right then,' Julie said. The cards might provide the guidance she needed.

Mark did Chris's reading first. There was a Two of Cups, a few Pentacles, a major arcana or two, including the Chariot. Julie always liked the design of the Chariot. She picked it up and studied it while Mark consulted his book and spoke of energy, and friends and feelings, and of money, and security to come. Mark finished Chris's reading. Chris felt that Mark's explanation of the cards had been most satisfactory.

'Your turn,' Simon said to Julie.

Julie wondered if Simon too was hoping the cards might suggest a course he couldn't navigate using his own outdated compass.

She took the cards, the big, colourful Waite pack so popular with her friends, and clumsily shuffled them. She returned the deck to Mark. He laid out the top ten cards in the Celtic Cross spread he favoured. He began to turn them over. The Lovers, the Two of Cups, the Wheel of Fortune, the Chariot, the four of Wands.

'So many major Arcana,' Simon said.

'Powerful stuff indeed,' Mark said.

Julie hardly needed Mark to tell her what all the cards meant. She could see it in the designs. So much love, cups exchanged, fingers entwined. Changes already made, and changes still to come. Comfort, home, geniality. The Sun. There had been so much sun. She picked up The Sun and looked at it, and then held it up to Simon.

'Our time,' Julie said. She wanted to laugh.

She put the card down, and found Simon's hand. She squeezed it. She bit the smile from her lips, but felt sure her eyes were unable to disguise it.

It was near the end of the reading. Mark turned over the last card.

In her future, the Page of Cups.

'Ah,' Mark said. 'Minor arcana.' He struggled for a meaning. He saw love, he said, and looked meaningfully, if slightly drunkenly towards Simon. But Simon was looking at the spread of cards. They all knew a little about the Tarot, they all had packs, it seemed – Nick, Simon, James and Imo and Stuart and Kate. Simon would also be interpreting the cards she had laid on the table.

'It's all about love,' Mark said. 'And change, of course. Love and change.' He lit a cigarette, and offered one to Julie. She took it, and Mark lit it for her.

She thanked him for the reading, but she knew the Page of Cups. Mark had been using as reference, The Tarot of the Bohemians. She liked the Page cards, and had read about them in the little booklet that came with the pack and contained A E Waite's interpretations of the symbols painted into the cards. The Pages were young men, messengers, and, yes, she knew she could be a romantic, but the Page of Cups was, according to Waite, a fair young man, who would render her service, and with whom she would be connected.

She did laugh then. The three young men who sat with her at the dining table looked across at her in surprise. 'Everything is

166

going to be fine,' she said. She put out her cigarette. She looked at Simon. 'I need to go home,' she said softly. 'And you need to walk me.'

She kissed Mark and Chris on the cheek, and then led Simon out through the front door, which Simon closed very gently behind him.

Julie and Simon walked along Barton Road. In ten minutes they would be in front of her door, and she knew now that she must say something about her thoughts to Simon. She lit another cigarette, breathed the smoke in deep and then blew it noisily into the sky.

'We've been great, haven't we?' Julie said.

It didn't matter what Simon said. She had listened to the cards. There were lovers, a fair-haired page, and the sharing of golden cups. Everything would be fine. Not now, although everything was fine, had been fine for weeks. But everything would be better in the future. She had only to navigate the shoals of now, and then, some when soon, not this week, not this month, and not even this year perhaps, but some when, there would be lovers, there would be cups full of emotion, there would be a fair-haired young man who would render her service.

'We have been great,' Simon agreed.

'But it has to stop now, Simon.'

'What? But... we're great. As you just said.'

'We are. But next weekend, I go to Swanage for two weeks with mum and dad and sis. And when I come back, we will still be friends. But all the kissing and the hugging has to stop.'

'But why?'

'Because I don't want to go any deeper only to hear you one day say, Anna is so sweet, Anna is gorgeous, what have I done?'

'But I like you!'

'I know you do. But you haven't seen Anna for ages. And I know that in the weeks before we started hanging around with each other, all you could think about was seeing her again. I heard that from Nick and Mark. When we got together, I was talking about Tim, and you were talking about Anna. And that was okay, you know, because we were just two old friends from school messing about together. But now... I have to know how you feel. And I can't, not until you've seen Anna again, and *you* know how you feel. Because waiting with that hanging over me will sour everything. It will ruin this, all of this.' Julie waved her arms about her. 'All this glorious sun, and light, and heat, and blue and beauty.' She looked across at Simon, then. 'Do you know what I mean? Do you?'

'Yes, of course,' Simon said. He was looking down at the dusty pavement.

Julie wondered what he was thinking. What if he broke through that reserve of his, that fear, that shyness, and suddenly said that he loved her? What would she do, what would become of her recent resolution?

They walked on a few more paces, and she knew then that Simon couldn't say anything, not yet. He *wasn't* ready. And she didn't mind at all. Because this was how it *must* be. She *must* be certain.

They arrived at Julie's house, and walked up the drive to the front door.

'We can still see each other, though,' Simon said.

'Of course we can. We're still friends. But things will change a little after the summer. You'll be at Southleigh, and I'll be at Salisbury Tech. I work as well. Things will be less intense, I think. But we'll still be there for each other. And I'll be in the Lion much more now. I've missed all you guys.'

'I have some have things to do next week. A tai chi class, kung fu as well. I need to do some work for college.'

Bless him, Julie thought. He knew what she meant. He knew what they had to do. *And I've had a Tarot reading.* 'We'll see each other tomorrow night, though,' she said.

'We will.'

'We'll go for a walk after the pub. I'd like that.'

'Of course. So would I.'

She put her arms around him then. She was safe here. There was something relaxing about Simon's hugs. 'You're really good at this.' These intimate embraces would need to stop. She would miss them.

Simon kissed her cheek. She knew he wanted to kiss her on the lips. And she wanted him to do it. Kissing Simon at Mark's party had been so very pleasant. Instead she squeezed him tighter, and was gratified to be squeezed back. They stayed like that for some time. Finally, they broke apart.

'Night, Simon.'

'Goodnight, Jules.'

She watched him walk down the driveway. This was the way things had to be. She was happy as she opened the door.

10

This is How it Ends

QUEEN of CUPS.

Simon called on Julie, and they walked down to the White Lion together. Simon didn't take her hand as he might have done two weeks ago. He was confused, but still happy to be sharing time with her. He hadn't shared this much time with a girl since Anna before the summer, or Angie and Sally during last year's summer. He thought they had enjoyed their time with him. He thought Julie had. Yet Angie and Sally now had boyfriends, boyfriends that were not him. He didn't understand anything, really. He knew he liked these moments with Julie, those moments with the others, knew that they made life happier and full of unexplored potentialities.

He should have said something to Julie, a couple of weeks ago perhaps, about how much he liked her. But he had been, as usual, unsure how to make that happen, hadn't wanted to just blurt something out, something that would sound silly and embarrassing when he remembered it later. Who said what to whom and when remained a mystery. He was afraid he would be rebuffed. *Always.* That was how he felt about the others – that they had enjoyed his company, but then chosen somebody else. And, judging by last night's conversation he had been right to be wary of *this*. He wasn't sure whether Julie liked him and couldn't cope with the Anna problem, or was just using that situation as a way to slip out of this friendship, relationship – or whatever it was – and find somebody less troublesome.

But it couldn't be the latter. No two people could be more genial than he and Julie had been this summer. Of that he was sure. He just didn't *know*. Was this his fate? To never understand? He would accept everything that was offered, and go with the flow. One day, somehow, he might finally mouth some words that would be understood by somebody else he had spent genial time with, and then their lives would intertwine in even deeper ways.

The saloon bar at the White Lion was surprisingly full for a Sunday night. Everyone was there, this summer's stars: Nick and Heather, Mark and Gaz, Chrissie and Jake, Steve, Danny, Stuart, Kate, and Imogen. And then there was Sarah, Angie, Sally, and all the friends of friends that spun out from there. Everyone was there except, of course, James. Imogen, Stuart and Kate sat close to each other. Imogen's face remained sad, her eyes puffy. She hadn't slept much. What Mark had said last night was right; you didn't know what would happen in the future, and James's disappearance confirmed that. Seize the day! Risk all! You only live once! Yet, even knowing today could be his last, Simon was aware that if he said the wrong thing he would still have to live his last few hours in embarrassment, curled up on a floor somewhere, hiding his head in shame or weeping. Those vividly imagined few hours of embarrassment were a stronger deterrent than the impetus to action of a barely-imagined calamity.

After the pub, Simon and Julie went to Mark's with Nick, Heather and Gaz for some more drinks and coffee and chat. They said goodbye to Mark at close to midnight.

'So, what about that walk?' Julie said.

'I'd love to,' Simon said.

Julie slipped an arm through Simon's. 'Let's find some grass to sit on.'

Simon suspected this might be the last time for a while, or perhaps forever, they would walk the hills in the genial way they had done over the last few weeks. It would certainly be the last walk they would have in this warmth, in this balmy, sultry air, he felt sure. It was hard to imagine that this weather could last very much longer; the rains must soon come and wash all this away, wash away everything except all the memories.

Simon led them southward. He knew the paths well enough now to follow them in the dark. He was heading for Up the Leg and Down the Stocking. They talked about poor Imogen, about Stuart and Kate, and Heather and Nick. Proper relationships, unlike the one he seemed to be involved in. On an impulse he put an arm across Julie's shoulders. He left his arm there as they walked the paths. She didn't shake it off. They talked about the ghost, and James. Finally, half way up the slope of Up the Leg and Down the Stocking they stopped, and sat on the grass. From here, they could see the orange and yellow town lights ahead of them, gently twinkling through the thin haze of the humid night. They lay on their backs and looked up at the stars studding the sky.

'Do *you* think we've been abducted,' Julie said.

'I don't think so,' Simon said.

'What about that ghost though? Do you think I saw a ghost?'

'You saw it. You know what you felt. I didn't see it, so I can't say what you saw.'

Julie took Simon's hand for a moment. 'I want it to be a

ghost. It *has* been a summer of wonders. There should be a ghost, and flying saucers, and telepathy.'

Simon dared lift Julie's hand to his lips, and kissed it. He suspected this would be the last kiss. Her hand smelled of soap. He remembered a few weeks ago, when all this had started, when he had enjoyed the scents of soap and shampoo and sweet tobacco on her. 'You smell nice,' he said. He placed her hand back on the grass beside them, and let go of it, but he continued to gently stroke the back of it with his fingers. It was as if they were slowly unweaving the physical connections they had made. This would be, he knew, their last intimacy of the summer.

'It's Astral soap,' Julie said.

'How apt,' Simon said. 'You're pure enough for the Astral Plane.'

'What *is* the Astral Plane?'

Simon shrugged. He'd never really given it much thought. 'A kind of intermediate place, between worlds. You can visit it, some say, by astral projection, whatever that is. It is *not* throwing a bar of soap at it.'

'I could manage that kind of astral projection.'

'I'm sure you could *try*. But you're a girl, so try as you might the soap would never reach.'

'How do you know? It could be all around us.'

Simon laughed, even though there was an air of solemnity about the evening. He would miss Julie. They would be friends, yes, of course they would, but things would be different. The summer would be over, the rain would arrive, with grey clouds and wind, and they would be mere friends again, chatting in the pub. Perhaps Julie would find somebody else. But he thought he understood.

As if reading his mind, Julie said, 'You should go for it with Anna. You really should.' She paused. 'She's right, you *are* very lovely.'

Simon didn't know what to think, what to do.

~ooo~

174

Julie felt acceptance in Simon's moments of silence, even though his fingers still gently, tenderly moved over the back of her hand, in what would be the last connection to be broken.

'You should go for it with Anna. You really should. She's right, you *are* lovely.'

And even then a finger continued tracing faint lines of connection across her hand.

'We can't carry on like this, Simon. I don't know what I want,' she lied. 'But your Anna, she sounds lovely.'

'I know,' Simon said. 'We'll always be friends, though, won't we? We can laugh.'

'Yes. Always there for each other.'

Julie looked into the sky, at the stars. They would always be friends, and they would always have this perfect summer. She studied the stars, and wondered if they were above or below the Astral Plane.

'I understand,' Simon said, 'Really.'

'Good.'

She wondered if he did, really, and if he would be hurt by the distance that would open between them after tonight. But he would be fine. Simon was nice. He was lovely. He was *her* Simon.

And in that moment of knowing, of release, of detachment, the stars brightened, glowed anew through the material of the Plane high and invisible over her. She squeezed Simon's hand then, quickly, one last physical intensity in their gossamer love, and then released it. Still a gentle finger traced lines, creating and maintaining that last connection.

And though Julie knew the stars were distant, still she believed she could reach out and touch them, hold their glitter to her. The spaces between the stars were empty, like black velvet, so dark, yet the whole sky held so many possibilities. She could feel each blade of grass beneath her hands as she stopped herself falling into the sky, the hands that Simon said were scented with Astral soap, and out there, out in the deep dark night, was what? The Astral Plane, aliens? She wanted there to be some reason for all this beauty. She loved Simon, she loved Sarah, and Imo and Mark and James, all of them, all of the stars that occupied her universe, she loved that Simon's touch was there, on her hand, at her wrist again, she knew there was no pressure on her, no pressure to perform, to be anyone, to be something or somebody she didn't want to be even out here, lying on the grass, on a sultry night, she knew Simon would do nothing now, not now they had talked, but there would always be this night and the days and nights that had led to it, there would always be a Simon somewhere inside her, in her soul, in the memory of long hot days, and car rides with Gray and Chris, Stonehenge, the smoking Mini, the fire brigade, Beacon Hill, and Nick and Stu and Imo and poor lost James and all the rest of them all jumbled into blue and heat. Part of her would always be a hot July day, bright and full of golden sun, always hovering in these same blue-hazed distances, simply drifting far enough to rediscover her position here looking inward and outward, negotiating dream and desires, friendship and love, looking back towards this simple place of bright sunlight, the Plain around her, these hills and downs, this town, and here and now on *this* grass with Simon and his gentle touch on the back of her hand. Somewhere in these dreams, an old house, outside, inside, beneath the curving vault of heaven, a house she had seen somewhere in the leaf-shaded sun, the inside outside house, a picture on the wall and yellow sunshine falling through the windows onto a table with flowers and across a tiled floor. And her feelings now – here, eyes closed, under the stars, Simon close to her – were warm, joyous, and full, and filled the hot, honeyed world around her with love and pleasure and she knew already that in the time to come and in the time that would pass there would be this forever moment when she opened up to the world, to the universe, to some god, and all of this, all this new realm, all the world and universe she had discovered this summer, all its very essence was here, now, because she smelt of Astral soap, because there had been a ghost, because there was another hand, because the stars shone and danced, because, for long, hot, bright, hazy days, there had been Simon and Julie

Julie's Tarot Spread

The playlist for courting
Year of the Cat – Al Stewart
Dancing Queen – Abba
You Make Me Feel Like Dancing – Leo Sayer
Play that Funky Music White Boy – Wild Cherry
Dancing in the Moonlight – King Harvest
Afternoon Delight – Starlight Vocal Band
I'm Mandy, Fly Me – 10cc
January – Pilot
Mississippi – Pussycat
S-S-S-Single Bed – Fox
Guitar Man – Bread
Sara Smile – Hall and Oates
At Seventeen – Janis Ian
Show Me the Way – Peter Frampton
Rock On – David Essex
48 Crash – Suzi Quatro
Ventura Highway – America
Drive in Saturday – David Bowie
The King Will Come – Wishbone Ash
I'm Not in Love – 10cc
Heaven Must be Missing an Angel – Tavares
Make it With You – Bread

The playlist for walking
Romance – Gerald Finzi
A Gloucestershire Rhapsody – Ivor Gurney
A Song of Summer – Frederick Delius
Eclogue for Piano and Strings – Gerald Finzi
Five Variants of Dives and Lazarus – Ralph Vaughan Williams
The Banks of Green Willow – George Butterworth
Tintagel – Arnold Bax
Serenade for Strings – Edward Elgar
Elegy for Viola, String Quartet and String Orchestra –
Herbert Howells

Hammersmith

The name exists in the Wiltshire landscape as an abandoned village
to the east of the A350, south of Warminster. Its state of ruin was
based on the villages of Snap and Imber, both also in Wiltshire.

http://www.abandonedcommunities.co.uk/snap.html
http://www.abandonedcommunities.co.uk/imber.html